THE TEN

Tender-hearted Nurse Juliet Reed intends devoting her life to caring for the sick. Why then do thoughts of the handsome, brilliant young surgeon Brook Wentworth fill not only her dreams but every waking moment?

*Books you will enjoy
in our Doctor–Nurse series*

THE TENDER HEART

BY

HAZEL FISHER

MILLS & BOON LIMITED
London · Sydney · Toronto

First published in Great Britain 1982
by Mills & Boon Limited, 15–16 Brook's Mews,
London W1A 1DR

ISBN 0 263 73811 6

03/0382/

Set in 10 on 12pt Times

Photoset by Rowland Phototypesetting Ltd.,
Bury St Edmunds, Suffolk.
Made and printed in Great Britain by
Richard Clay (The Chaucer Press) Ltd.,
Bungay, Suffolk

CHAPTER ONE

It was chilly in the corridor leading from the training school to the main hospital. Student Nurse Juliet Reed shivered in the thin white uniform, though more from a kind of dreadful anticipation than from the October cold.

Her sapphire-blue eyes were sad as she glanced at the others from her set all gaily talking. As the daughter of a senior and much-respected consultant she was automatically set apart, and her shy, retiring nature completed her isolation.

Introductory Block was almost over. Now at last they were to become *real* nurses. True, during their weeks in training school they had visited the wards almost daily for short periods, but today was different; they were to spend an entire shift on the wards to which they had been allocated.

Juliet's ward was Arndale, female surgical, where, starting next Monday, she would spend eight weeks. Today was a preliminary trial. She was glad it was surgery first. At least it wouldn't be her father's ward. After Arndale she would be allocated to a geriatric ward, then her first spell of night duty.

Miss Matthews' thin, angular figure hove into view, and the group obediently fell into place behind her. Miss Matthews was their clinical instructor, one of four at the District General Hospital at Garnhill-on-Sea—D.G.H.

for short. It was a huge, modern, pale-grey building, so big that Juliet was convinced she would never find her way about the endless corridors.

She nibbled her lower lip anxiously, feeling much younger than her nineteen years. With her silky, chestnut hair, small regular features and delicate bone structure, she looked younger as well. The sparse but notice-able dusting of freckles on her pert little nose didn't help. Hardly the portrait of a calm, efficient nurse, she mused, sadly, then heard the girl behind her mutter.

Juliet turned and smiled tentatively at Elma Graham, the tall black student, who was examining a hole in her tights. That black tights looked incongruous with white uniform appeared to have escaped the notice of those responsible, but on Elma, of course, they were just right. Juliet was tempted to say so but feared a rebuff.

Elma returned her smile, big white teeth flashing, and Juliet felt immensely better. Perhaps she wasn't quite alone, after all. But she was surprised when Elma moved nearer and whispered that she was half-inclined to run if the surgical sister proved to be a dragon!

There was no time for further conversation as they approached Arndale, where Juliet and Elma were both to work.

Miss Matthews introduced them to Staff Nurse Roberts then disappeared with the rest of her brood, leaving the ill-at-ease girls to loiter outside the office while Sister Paice took the hand-over.

To Juliet, this wasn't nursing at all. She certainly hadn't come just to hang around idly, so, feeling self-conscious, she walked over to the nearest patient and smiled shyly.

The woman beamed at her, then said smugly: 'Ah! you'll be first-year, then! I can see by your white belt.'

Juliet nodded, pleased. 'We all wear the same uniform and plain caps, as you've seen, but next year Elma and I will get light blue belts because we will be second-year.'

The patient, Mrs Simmonds, nodded, then smiled coyly at someone behind the girls.

Juliet's heart missed a beat. A doctor! A real doctor and not a nurse in sight except themselves.

'Mr Wentworth! Don't say we rate *two* visits today!' Mrs Simmonds put in, and some of the frozen inertia left Juliet—to be replaced by sheer panic. She'd heard of Mr Brook Wentworth, who was a young but highly regarded consultant surgeon, a demi-god. He would expect them to know about the patients! Swiftly the panic subsided as Juliet's commonsense came to the fore. She must summon Sister Paice.

'Excuse me, sir. I'll fetch Sister . . .' Juliet began, but the tall, dark-haired consultant made an impatient gesture.

'You can attend to me. Sister is always busy at this time.'

'We can't!' Elma's chuckle caused Mr Wentworth to swing round, and Juliet closed her eyes and offered up a short prayer. 'Can't' was a word junior nurses did not use to consultants!

The surgeon evidently thought so too. 'Nonsense!' he snapped, then flicked his dark glance in Juliet's direction. She experienced a sense of shock as the black eyes bored fiercely into her own and, for a second, was conscious of nothing else. The ward, the patients,

Elma—they all disappeared and there were only two people left in the whole world.

A puzzled expression showed briefly on his face as though he shared Juliet's peculiar feeling, then, irritably, he dismissed her: 'You can make me some coffee, young lady!'

Juliet's mouth opened to protest, but Mr Wentworth had already turned to Elma, presumably thinking her the more capable of the two.

Annoyed, but secretly relieved to escape from him, Juliet hurried out to find the ward kitchen. She had never been on Arndale before, but most of the words followed the same pattern and she found it easily.

Doctors were supposed to use the staff canteen but she didn't feel up to telling Mr Wentworth that. Juliet put the kettle on to boil with hands that shook a little. Reaction, she told herself, sternly. Sheer fright because she'd thought Mr Wentworth was going to ask her questions about the patient.

But reasoning did not help. Although she accepted that she looked about fifteen, she *was* a calm capable girl, not given to panics. No, it was those eyes—like living coals in the surgeon's lean, pale face, she thought fancifully, then nearly jumped out of her skin when a cold, female voice spoke: 'And just *what* do you think you're doing, Nurse?'

A tall, well-built blonde wearing a Ward Sister's lace cap strode in, and Juliet mentally quailed, but she met the Sister's gaze with a smile. 'I'm Student Nurse Reed, please Sister. From Introductory Block. Nurse Graham and I are here for the afternoon, until nine-thirty. Mr Wentworth asked for coffee,' she went on, her tiny smile fading. It seemed as if Sister Paice was going to be the dragon Elma had feared.

Cool, pale blue eyes took stock of Juliet, and from Sister's expression she didn't think much of what she saw. 'Never mind. Get Mr Wentworth his coffee and bring it in. He likes it strong and sweet. And a cup for me, please.' Sister disappeared before Juliet could recover her wits, and with lips pressed tightly together, she did as she was bid. So, he liked it strong and sweet, did he?

Aware that she was courting disaster, she deliberately put in only half a teaspoon of instant coffee, added just sufficient water to mix it then filled the cup with hot milk. Today Mr High and Mighty was having weak coffee!

Juliet made Sister's coffee stronger, then, a search of the cupboard having revealed nothing in the way of biscuits or cakes, she carried the coffee into the office. The door was ajar and she could see Sister deep in conversation with the consultant. At least she supposed it was conversation. Sister's blonde curly head was bent towards him, and Juliet heard a muted giggle, then saw Sister draw one finger teasingly down the side of the consultant's face.

Eyebrows arched in disgust, Juliet marched in after a perfunctory knock. Ignoring the two by the big desk, she placed the tray on one corner of it, then hurried out, head held high. If they wanted to carry on when they should be healing the sick, it was no concern of hers. It didn't matter a scrap.

The sick feeling in the pit of her stomach told her it *did* matter. It mattered a lot, she told herself, as she went in search of Elma. Affairs went on during duty-hours as well as off-duty.

Dedication. There isn't much of *that* around these days, her father had told her. She'd protested, refusing to discard her vision of all senior nurses as carbon-copies of Florence Nightingale; of doctors as dedicated, selfless gods.

'Doctors and nurses are human beings.' Juliet could see her father's face as he'd said that. He looked sad, a little ashamed, perhaps, that he'd been the one to strip the scales from her eyes. To her it was clear-cut. You became a nurse because you wanted to heal the sick. That nurses and doctors were often ambitious, ruthless in their desire to scale the ladder of promotion, simply had not occurred to the unworldly Juliet.

Elma was with a nursing auxiliary. They were playing Scrabble in the dayroom with two up patients. The auxiliary, Pam Noble, assured Juliet there was nothing else to be done at present, but Juliet fretted, knowing she ought to find the Staff Nurse and make sure for herself. 'What did Mr Wentworth say to you?' she asked, suddenly remembering Elma's ordeal.

Her colleague rolled her eyes in an exaggerated fashion. 'It was awful, Juliet! He snapped and growled, just like some animal in a cage!'

Juliet's soft mouth curved into a smile and she was about to comment when she found Sister Paice beside her.

'When you young girls have finished fooling around, you can come to my office!' she said tersely, then apparently changed her mind. 'You, Nurse,' indicating Elma, 'can get on with the bedpans. Someone might want one. You,' an airy gesture from the slim, elegant hand indicated Juliet, 'can come into the office. Mr Wentworth has something to say to you.'

Sister hurried away and poor Juliet followed slowly. Much more slowy. It must be the coffee. Mr Wentworth was angry because it was so weak. Surely her crime was no greater than that?

He was small-minded, that's what he was. Yet Brook Wentworth was one person on whom her father lavished unqualified praise. Young, up and coming, and brilliant, Dr Reed called him. Well, if he was petty enough to tear strips off a young nurse because the coffee wasn't to his liking, she wanted none of him. The next time Father praised Mr Wentworth she would put him in the picture.

Trying desperately to pretend she hadn't a care in the world, Juliet followed Sister Paice into the big, well-equipped office.

Mr Wentworth was perched on a corner of the desk, long legs swinging idly. Close to, he seemed younger. And pale, the only colour coming from his dark, feverishly-bright eyes. He looked desperately tired, and Juliet's eyes softened.

'This is one of the nurses, Mr Wentworth,' Sister said tartly, standing aside so that the full weight of the surgeon's wrath could fall on Juliet.

His dark hair was thick. So were his brows, really bushy, Juliet noticed, before Mr Wentworth spoke: 'When a surgeon asks a nurse to assist with a patient the last thing he expects is rudeness, Nurse.' The words, though softly-spoken, shocked Juliet, and she coloured fiercely.

'W . . . what rudeness, sir?' she stammered, and heard Sister's shocked gasp behind her.

The surgeon raised those bushy brows Juliet had previously found so fascinating. 'Are you suggesting you and your colleague were in any way *helpful*?' Mr Wentworth sounded scandalised, and Juliet just stood, rooted to the spot. Surely she hadn't been unhelpful?

'But I . . . we didn't know any of the patients,' she began, then Sister mercifully stepped in, with a warm smile for the consultant.

'I'm sure Nurse didn't intend any disrespect, Mr Wentworth. She's very young.' She frowned at Juliet as though it was her own fault that she was only nineteen.

Mr Wentworth grunted and that, apparently, was the end of the interview. Juliet swallowed nervously, wondering if Sister was going to start on her now, but her fears proved groundless. 'You can help the auxiliary, Nurse.' Sister Paice smiled almost kindly at her, but Juliet fled, her mind in a whirl. She had been carpeted for something she hadn't done, then, when she had expected a further verbal blow, Sister had been kind instead. No wonder she was confused! Mr Wentworth apparently considered the weak coffee the least of her crimes, so she ought to be grateful for that.

Although she couldn't put the consultant entirely from her mind she quickly became absorbed in the ward routine and it was time to go to supper before she knew it. Six-thirty already! She and Elma had survived six hours on Arndale and had not, so far, committed any major blunders. Apart, of course, from not being sufficient help to Mr Wentworth. Elma, Juliet noticed, was

not called into the ward-office and given the benefit of
the surgeon's opinion.

There were twenty-eight patients on Arndale, each
set of four beds curtained off to give the impression of
side-wards, though in fact Arndale, was one long ward,
with a small dayroom at the opposite end from the office.
The curtains gave the ladies some privacy, Juliet was
glad to see. Two years before, she'd had her appendix
removed whilst on holiday in the Midlands and her ward
had had no curtains, apart from those drawn when
patients were attending to personal functions; no parti-
tions—nothing except nearly forty beds in a long straight
line. The sort of ward where Miss Nightingale herself
would have felt at home. Juliet had been embarrassed at
the lack of privacy. Everywhere eyes had seemed to be
upon her, and there was no escape. She was glad to see
her very own ward wasn't like that.

She began to feel proud of Arndale Ward, to feel she
belonged. The D.G.H. was too new a hospital to have
traditions, for nurses and doctors to feel part of a fine old
institution, but Juliet was fiercely proud of being a nurse
there and felt the D.G.H. was as good as any of the
teaching hospitals. Even if the sense of dedication
among the staff was difficult to find at first, she was
convinced it was there. She would just have to dig
deeper, that was all.

While Elma was at first supper, Sister Paice had Juliet
in the office and gave her a brief rundown of the patients
on the ward. Juliet was nervous at first and felt trapped.
She hardly dared ask questions about the various dis-
orders, but eventually her enthusiasm proved stronger
than her diffidence and soon she and Sister were deep in

conversation, chatting away as though they were old friends. She wasn't a dragon emitting smoke, after all. Juliet excused Sister's earlier abruptness with the thought that because the consultant was angry, the ward sister had to be, too.

Juliet judged her to be about thirty, or a little less. She was tall and curvy, with short, curly blonde hair that showed faintly dark at the roots. Although Sister wasn't pretty her round face and light blue eyes were attractive, Juliet considered, generously. I wonder if Mr Wentworth fancies her, she mused idly, as Sister flicked through a textbook.

Juliet momentarily closed her eyes in horror. She was supposed to be listening and learning. Now just *how* did her thoughts come to be on the arrogant, bad-tempered consultant?

Sister's eyes narrowed. 'Something troubling you, Nurse?'

She doesn't miss a thing, Juliet thought, then shook her head decisively. 'Oh, no, Sister. My eyes are a bit tired, that's all.'

'Hm. There will be days when most of you is tired, Nurse. Not just your eyes! You'll be so bone-weary that all you will want to do is sleep for a week. Yet you will keep going because that's nursing.'

Juliet brightened. Sister Paice must be one of those dedicated nurses her father insisted did not exist. 'It will be very rewarding, Sister,' she ventured, sapphire eyes fixed on the older woman, above whose head Juliet's vivid imagination had fixed a halo.

Sister shrugged. 'Yes, but rewards take a long time and don't always go to those who deserve them. I shouldn't talk like this in front of you, Nurse Reed, but you seem a sensible young girl. I'm hoping for promotion next year. One rung further up the ladder.' Sister rose and smiled down at Juliet, who mentally snatched away the halo she had fancifully bestowed upon her senior.

Promotion! Was that all they thought about! Surely not?

Feeling young, gauche and very stupid, Juliet sadly went to her supper, still convinced that she would soon find some dedication on Arndale Ward.

After a further day in school and the weekend off, Juliet began work in earnest on Arndale Ward. Sister was right, there *were* days when Juliet felt she couldn't go on any longer, that she simply *must* sleep for twenty-four hours, but the weariness passed. By the end of her first week she had learned to trot around the ward whilst giving the impression of merely walking; to keep up with her seniors when making beds or giving bed-baths—and to stay discreetly out of the way whenever consultants did a round. One consultant in particular, anyway.

The ward was divided between Mr Wentworth and Mr Parker, who was nearing retirement and who always smiled at nurses, no matter how junior. Mr Wentworth could learn a few lessons from him, Juliet thought resentfully, still stinging from the icy look Mr Wentworth had bestowed upon her when they nearly collided in the office doorway. It wasn't Juliet's fault that he had arrived early. She wasn't supposed to be a mind-reader, surely?

It didn't take a lot of skill to read his mind when it

came to Sister Paice. He was besotted with her. Juliet could see that without the aid of a crystal ball. A faint smile hovered about his wide mouth when he reached the ward-office. Juliet had seen it at close quarters when he nearly knocked her down. At first, she'd thought the smile was for her. Then she realised—Mr Wentworth was on his way to visit his lady-love.

She often heard them laughing in the office. Mr Wentworth had a husky sort of chuckle, very sexy . . . The thermometer dropped from Juliet's suddenly weak fingers and broke.

Elma laughed. 'It isn't like you to drop things! Me, I'm the clumsy one!' She laughed again, clearly not bothered. Juliet envied the other girl her composure. Nothing worried Elma. It was obvious, even to Juliet, that Elma wasn't very efficient and made some awful mistakes. Yet the patients loved her and often she could coax them to take tablets or to drink the awful bowel-cleansing drink that Mr Parker prescribed for his patients. It took all sorts.

Staff Nurse Roberts, by comparison, was Miss Efficient herself. She never did anything wrong. Or, if she did, it was always someone else's fault. Quite often the victim was Juliet, as was the case now. She was due off at five before her two rest days, but because Staff Nurse had spent so long chatting to a colleague they were behind with essential work, and Juliet knew she wouldn't get away before six. Sister was off-duty or it would never have happened.

If it was an emergency Juliet would not have minded how long she had to work, would have stayed all night if need be, but she resented having to stay because of the

Staff Nurse's laziness. Mrs Roberts certainly wasn't in line for promotion, Juliet thought sourly, as she wearily tidied the cupboard in the clinic.

'I'm done!' Elma's voice broke into Juliet's thought. 'Will you be long, Juliet?'

Juliet shrugged. 'Probably. I'll see you on Tuesday. When are you off?'

'Tuesday! My days off are split this week. Be good until Wednesday. Bye!'

Juliet glanced at her fob-watch. Five exactly. Oh, well, she wasn't going anywhere. Elma, she knew, was going steady with one of the young porters so would be fully occupied on her days off. If their off-duty ever coincided, Juliet intended to invite Elma home to meet her father. After all, she was thousands of miles from home and must get lonely sometimes, though it was hard to believe that the happy, extrovert Elma could be lonely. Although she lived at home, Juliet was the lonelier of the two. When her mother died of cancer, Juliet, at fourteen, had been shipped off to boarding-school. Her father believed it would be for the best.

Much as Juliet loved her father, she secretly criticised his decision. It was made out of love for her, but had been misguided. Because boarding-school was the other side of London, and they lived in Sussex, she had no childhood friends to keep her company. No one of her age lived locally. Their house was on the outskirts of Garnhill and was a popular area for retirement.

Still, she would make friends eventually, she supposed. Yet, because of her father, the other students weren't keen to get to know Juliet, feeling that she considered herself a cut above them. That it was her natural diffidence never occurred to them. Only with Elma did she feel at ease.

Juliet swung around, suddenly aware of being watched. Dr O'Boyle, their Irish housedoctor, stood in the doorway, his smile wide and welcoming.

'Oh! Hello, Doctor. Shall I find Staff Nurse for you?'

Dr O'Boyle sighed, grey eyes sad. 'You always look so efficient and business-like, Nurse darling. Do you never have time for small-talk?' The huge, thin young doctor walked into the clinic, and Juliet met his gaze levelly. Charming and attractive though he was, he left her cold. He was a hard worker, she knew, and she'd been delighted to find that he had some of the dedication she had begun to despair of finding, but . . .

He sighed, a big, exaggerated sigh, and Juliet's lips quivered. Immediately he pounced on the gesture. 'See! You nearly smiled then, Nurse darling! If you ever laughed, why I'd start somersaulting all over the place!'

His engaging grin almost wore down Juliet's resistance, but she was too tired to exchange banter with him. 'I'm sorry, Doctor, but I have to get done.'

'Isn't that always the way? Must get done before the consultant's round. Must get done before supper. Must get . . .'

Juliet began to smile, her tiredness lifting a little, then the smile died on her face. Behind the young doctor a pair of black eyes held hers.

'What is it, my sweet young nurse?' Dr O'Boyle began, taking a step towards Juliet, who shrank back against the trolley.

'I'm afraid Sister is off today, sir,' Juliet said, loudly, and felt something of Dr O'Boyle's embarrassment as he swung round and met the cold, condemning gaze of his senior.

The doctors exchanged a few words while Juliet composed herself mentally. She wanted to straighten her cap, which she knew was crooked, but dare not. Mr Wentworth might think she and Dr O'Boyle had been fooling around.

Dr O'Boyle drifted away without a backward glance and Juliet was left with the consultant.

The dark eyes held hers and she was incapable of movement, drained of all resistance. It wasn't an unpleasant sensation, but it was unnerving. Her lips moved but no sound emerged.

Mr Wentworth needed a shave. His chin was dark in the pale face. He needs a holiday in the sunshine as well, Juliet decided, her tender heart going out to him. Hateful and proud though he was, he *did* work hard and his paleness was evidence of the hours he spent in theatre, saving lives.

'I came to see you, Nurse Reed,' he said, quietly, and Juliet's heart skipped a beat. He wanted to see *her*? She opened her mouth to speak but thought better of it. Never interrupt your seniors. So she waited, but apparently he had no more to say, as he glanced around the clinic as though he had never seen it before.

'Shouldn't you be on the ward?' he asked sharply, and Juliet's lips tightened. He was going to pick on her again!

'I'm not with the patients because . . .' she began. Because Staff Nurse has been wasting time this afternoon and I've had extra chores to do. Hardly! 'Because there is a lot of tidying to do, sir,' she finished, and he showed surprise.

'As a student you are here to learn. Tidying-up is a job for auxiliaries, surely? Never mind,' he waved away her explanation and, crossly, she closed her mouth.

A faint smile crossed his weary face. 'Your eyes are snapping at me, Nurse!'

Juliet reddened, struggling to control her temper. Indeed, she was remarkably even-tempered, but this man, knowingly or not, persisted in brushing her fur the wrong way. If she emerged from her stay on Arndale as a bad-tempered shrew, she would know who to blame!

'Come on then, get your things.' Mr Wentworth glanced at his watch. 'Thought you young girls finished at five.'

Juliet was struck dumb, but at last blurted out: 'I c . . . can't go yet, sir. I have to get done!' Helplessly, she indicated the supplies she was supposed to put away before reporting to Staff Nurse for further duties.

The consultant looked scandalised. 'Do you mean you expect me to wait about while you tidy up?'

'No, of course not!' Juliet said, crossly, then wished she hadn't.

Mr Wentworth's expression was positively evil now and Juliet felt cold and trembly. He would report her to Sister and possibly the P.N.O. herself! Her eyes widened in dismay. Surely she wouldn't be thrown out?

'What's the matter, Nurse?' He sounded concerned, and was beside her before she realised he had moved.

A gentle, capable hand tilted her chin, and Juliet was obliged to meet his gaze. His eyes, she found to her surprise, were not cold and disdainful after all. They were large and warm and tender, and Juliet found herself drowning in them.

CHAPTER TWO

'MORE tea, Wentworth?' Dr Stafford Reed indicated the priceless rose-patterned teapot, but Brook Wentworth shook his head, his eyes on Juliet, who sat a little apart from the men.

From her window-seat she could gaze out into the garden from time to time, or at the terrace—anything to keep her mind and eyes away from Mr Wentworth.

This was why he'd hurried her away. Unbeknown to his daughter, Dr Reed had invited Mr Wentworth to tea. Because of it, Juliet had to leave most of the tidying-up. Naturally, Staff Nurse Roberts had told her to go once she knew that a *consultant* was waiting for her. She had seemed a bit put-out, but it was Sister Paice's reaction that worried Juliet. She would be angry when she knew that Juliet had been whisked away by Mr Wentworth. Angry and perhaps jealous, believing that Juliet was encroaching on her patch.

Idly, Juliet stirred her tea, though it was cold and she wasn't thirsty anyway. The two doctors were talking shop now, lost in a world of their own. Juliet, the tea laid out invitingly on the trolley, the warm old house, nothing existed for them. Juliet half-listened to them, then stole a glance at the garden.

Darkness was falling. At the moment they were in a delicate half-light, neither day nor night. She ought to draw the gold velvet curtains, shut out the chill of the evening, but would not. Mr Wentworth might take it as a hint that he ought to be going. Dr Reed had assured him he was welcome to stay for dinner, but Mr Wentworth, it seemed, had a previous engagement. With Sister Paice? Juliet wondered.

Where would he take her? There was not many interesting eating-places hereabouts. In Garnhill itself there was a splendid Chinese restaurant, and one or two hotels which catered for non-residents. Nowhere exciting, though, as far as she knew. Perhaps they would drive up to London. No, he would be too tired.

While the men were discussing things medical, Juliet decided it was safe enough to look at Mr Wentworth. The consultant fitted in well. He appeared at ease in their gracious sitting-room surrounded by antiques and rich carpets. He lounged comfortably in the huge, wine-coloured velvet armchair beside the roaring log fire. The dark suit was immaculate, his shirt spotless white, tie a discreet maroon. She glanced at his highly-polished shoes. Every inch the successful surgeon.

Evidently he came from a moneyed family. Juliet's father was gregarious and often invited younger doctors for a meal, and so many of them appeared ill-at-ease in the opulence of the house, but not Brook Wentworth. He belonged here at Five Gables.

They had driven down in silence, Mr Wentworth having apparently promised Juliet's father he would give her a lift home. How he must have hated it!

Juliet wished she could join in the conversation. She could not really talk shop with them, not after only one week as a nurse! And small talk had always been beyond her. She was trapped in her own little shell and could only gaze out, wistfully, knowing full well that she would retreat if Mr Wentworth *did* deign to speak to her.

He had shed his tiredness, she was relieved to see, though there were deep lines around his eyes and mouth. Lines Juliet wanted desperately to smooth away. His face was lean and hard, his chin stubborn. He wasn't exactly handsome, but those eyes! They were big, black and lustrous under long curling lashes. Juliet envied him those black eyes. She considered her own dark blue eyes very ordinary, unaware that they were sapphire-blue, and that her pale lashes were tipped with gold, or that her long, wavy, chestnut hair became a flaming halo of deep gold and copper when the light caught it.

No, Juliet Reed was very, very ordinary and certainly the sooner she stopped her fanciful imaginings about the debonair consultant, the better. She rose, unwilling to disturb the men, yet anxious to put as much space between her and Mr Wentworth as possible. About to mutter some excuse about having to study, she was stopped in her tracks by her father's next words:

'And Gemma?' How is she these days? Still the same, I suppose?'

Mr Wentworth stared into the fire. 'Yes, still the same. Still beautiful. And still very sure this time she will make it.'

Dr Reed grunted, and Juliet's gaze went from one to the other. She didn't think this Gemma was a patient, it appeared to be a mutual friend they were discussing. And Mr Wentworth seemed despondent about her. She hovered, uncertainly, but neither man realised she had moved.

'What will you do about her, Wentworth?' her father asked.

Brook Wentworth lifted one shoulder in a helpless gesture, and Juliet wanted to run to him. He got up and stood, hands in trouser pockets, staring down at the logs which spluttered and cracked at his feet.

'I don't know. I'm nearly at my wits' end! She's so young and lovely. Perhaps it would be easier if she was a stranger, someone I could cure with the knife! If only I wasn't so fond of her,' he finished, quietly, and Juliet felt as though Mr Wentworth's knife was in her, cutting out her heart.

He was fond of this Gemma. She was young and lovely—and sick. He loved her. His whole demeanour suggested that. The man was being torn apart because he could not help her, could not cure whatever illness she had. Perhaps she was a child? Juliet thought, hopefully, then discarded the idea. Gemma could be his sister, though. *That* was a reasonable explanation. Juliet brightened. Gemma was his sister and he was understandably concerned about her.

At last Mr Wentworth appeared to notice Juliet and sent a vague smile in her direction as she hovered, faintly bewildered. She doubted that he actually saw her, as a person, that was. She was simply someone to whom he had to be polite because she was Dr Reed's daughter.

'Ah, going out, Juliet?' Her father suddenly remembered he had a daughter.

Numbly she shook her head, then blushed fiercely as her father went on, tactlessly: 'If I were twenty years younger I would take you out myself!'

Juliet wanted to shake him, more so when she caught

the surgeon's eye. There was a gleam there, whether of mirth or malice she wasn't sure, but he was clearly enjoying her discomfiture.

Horrid man! Just because it was nearing the weekend and she was all alone he thought it funny. He was horrid, hateful, arrogant . . . She ran out of adjectives and merely gave him a polite but meaningless smile as she wished him goodnight.

Mr Wentworth held out his hand and Juliet had no option. She didn't want to touch him, remembering too well how she'd felt when he touched her in the clinic; the pleasurable sensation when his cool fingers gently tilted her head back. Those same fingers had glided along and dwelt for a moment on the sensitive spot behind her ear.

She hoped he would assume her flushed face was due to the warmth of the room as their hands touched, briefly. She almost snatched hers away as a flame shot up her arm, yet he appeared to feel nothing.

Then he was gone, in a hurry to get to Sister Paice, no doubt, Juliet thought.

At dinner, served as usual by Dr Reed's housekeeper, Muriel Snowden, Juliet tentatively brought up the subject of the mysterious Gemma. She simply had to know or there would be no sleep for her that night.

'That's an unusual name. Gemma, I mean,' she said, artlessly, flicking a quick look at her father.

Dr Reed's blue eyes met his daughter's. 'I didn't realise you were listening,' he commented mildly, pushing away his soup-plate.

'I couldn't help hearing, Father. Is . . . is she very ill?'

'Depends what you call ill, I suppose,' was the irritatingly vague reply, and Juliet tried a different tactic.

'He must be worried about her. About his sister, I mean.'

'Sister? Whose sister?'

'This Gemma. From the serious expression on his face I assumed she was a relation, his sister, probably.' There, at last, she's got the question out.

'You noticed his expression, then?'

'Father!' Juliet bit her lip in annoyance, causing her father to chuckle.

Carefully, he dabbed at his greying moustache with his napkin. 'Delicious soup, that. I wonder what Muriel puts in it?'

Juliet pushed her barely tasted soup away. 'I thought it a bit too salty, but she knows you enjoy heavily seasoned food,' she said wanly, stacking the dishes preparatory to wheeling them out. She wasn't the tiniest bit hungry but would try to eat most of the main course so as not to offend Mrs Snowden.

'Juliet.'

Stubbornly, she finished arranging the dishes on the trolley before glancing up. 'Yes?'

'Gemma isn't Brook's sister. She isn't any blood relation at all.' Her father's gaze was pitying as it rested on her, and the crocks rattled as Juliet hurried out, not wanting to hear any more.

Tuesday was Mr Wentworth's operating day. During her first week Juliet hadn't been involved very much in the preparation of patients for theatre, but now she was to learn to make up a bed for a patient returning from theatre. The various beds, operation, amputation and so on, had been demonstrated during Introductory Block, naturally, and Juliet had taken her turn at practising the various types. Making them up on the ward proved more difficult, though, particularly when they were pressed for time.

Sister Paice was her instructor, though how the woman found time from her own duties Juliet would never know. Juliet was on early duty, which commenced at seven-thirty, yet Sister was there before her, busily preparing her ward.

Juliet thought Sister gave her a rather strained smile, so perhaps she had heard that Mr Wentworth had driven her home. He may even have mentioned it himself. Seemingly she did not attach any importance to the matter and Juliet breathed freely again.

She had just finished making the bed to Sister's satisfaction when Dr O'Boyle breezed into the ward.

'Morning, Sister darling! And Nurse dear!'

Sister Paice gave him a dignified smile. 'You are early for once. Mustn't keep Mr Wentworth waiting. Would you look at Mrs Hollebon?'

Dr O'Boyle stood, humming good-naturedly, while Sister went to fetch Mrs Hollebon's notes, then he winked at Juliet as she pushed the linen-skip. 'Now there's a lovely lady for you! Calm, gracious, not a bad-looker, either.'

'Why don't you blind her with you charm, then?' Juliet asked innocently, her mind on her work, but his reply quickly caught her attention.

'Because I have no wish to live dangerously or die young, Nurse dear,' the young doctor said, solemnly. 'I'm not trespassing on Mr Wentworth's private residence. Him and Sister are like that, if you know what I mean.' Dr O'Boyle crossed his fingers and legs, and shot Juliet a knowing look.

Nodding to indicate that she understood perfectly, Juliet glided away. Yes, she did know what he meant. Sister Paice was Mr Wentworth's private property. They were lovers. She didn't need Dr O'Boyle to spell it out for her.

The day lost its appeal after that and nothing seemed to go right. Just after lunch, Mrs Clarke, a patient on women's medical, died, and Sister asked Juliet to assist with last offices. Sister was keen that all first-years should learn to cope with that task, even if it mean assisting on another ward.

'Have you ever seen a dead body, Nurse?' she asked, kindly, and her sigh of relief was audible when Juliet nodded.

'My mother died at home. She wanted to die in her own bed,' Juliet whispered, forlornly, then quickly pulled herself together. 'I . . . I didn't help with her, though. I helped nurse her in the last weeks, but not at the end,' she faltered.

'There isn't anything very difficult about it, Nurse. And dead people are in no way frightening. To perform last offices on a patient you have nursed is a privilege— the last service you are able to peform for him or her. If you think about it that way, it becomes easier.'

Juliet nodded, blue eyes serious. It was all part of nursing, wasn't it? Part of that dedication to duty she strived for.

She was glad that Mrs Clarke hadn't been Mr Wentworth's patient, though to a doctor or surgeon an occasional death was part of the day's work, she supposed.

They could not expect *all* their patients to recover.

Juliet was to assist a Nurse Prior with the task. Nurse Prior wasn't a lot older than her, and was a plodding, methodical sort of girl who apparently saw no reason to explain anything to Juliet as they worked.

Beyond terse requests for items from the trolley, Nurse Prior worked in silence, while Juliet fretted inwardly. It was ridiculous to think they should talk to the patient as they were taught to do when giving a bedbath, but Juliet felt some conversation was called for. Although used to quietness, the enforced silence now was getting on her nerves. She felt guilty and embarrassed, but she did long for the procedure to be over. Probably her next last offices wouldn't affect her at all. She was being over-emotional and selfish. If Nurse Prior didn't complain, why should she?

At last the card giving details of the patient was attached to the mortuary sheet and the S.E.N. indicated that Juliet could pack up and remove the trolley.

In her hurry to get away from the scene Juliet skidded, then ran the trolley into the tall figure of Mr Wentworth, against whom it came to rest.

White and shaken, Juliet gaped up at him, an apology trembling on her lips. Beside him stood a Staff Nurse and she proceeded to give Juliet a dressing-down before the apology left her lips.

'That will *do*, Staff!' The surgeon spoke softly, but Staff Nurse stopped immediately.

Tears sprang to Juliet's eyes and hastily she blinked them away before pulling the trolley back a little. 'I'm really very sorry, sir,' she whispered, then quickly manoeuvred the trolley past the two of them before realising, to her horror, that she was going in the wrong direction. Sight of the dreaded Mr Wentworth on a strange ward had completely unnerved her.

Embarrassed, and knowing that she might be sick any moment, Juliet changed direction, certain that all eyes were upon her as she hastened away.

Five o'clock came eventually, and a wan and tired Juliet walked home. Fortunately, Five Gables was only fifteen minutes brisk walk from the hospital, but Juliet felt anything but brisk, and it was nearly six when she wearily pushed open the white gates and crunched up the short drive. Occasionally her father was able to give her a lift home, but it wasn't often that their duties coincided.

She continued to dawdle as she let herself in the side-door. She was a failure, she would never become a nurse. Nothing mattered any more . . .

'Ah! Thought I heard you, Juliet.' Her father's deep tones were, for once, unwelcome. She needed to be alone.

'I'll just change and be down in a while, Father,' she began, then caught her breath. Brook Wentworth appeared in the sitting-room doorway.

For a moment she thought he had come to demand an apology for her stupidity that afternoon, then dismissed the idea. He would have seen her in the ward-office or got Sister Paice to tell her off.

'We have a guest for dinner, dear, so hurry down once you've changed,' Dr Reed said mildly, well aware that the biddable Juliet would obey him.

She clenched her fists, wishing she could escape, wishing for once that she *wasn't* docile, obedient, biddable. She was a person, not the dainty little doll her father believed her to be. Juliet wanted to cry, to scream, to beat her hands upon the door in a rage.

But the rebellious feeling passed, and Juliet muttered assent, then hurried up to wash and change. How she was to sit through a whole evening of the surgeon's company she didn't know, yet somehow it had to be endured. She hoped her father would not drop any more broad hints about her having no one to take her out for the evening.

Fresh and cool after her bath, Juliet made her way very slowly to the sitting-room. She had forgone her usual light tea because she wanted to spend as little time as possible with Mr Wentworth. She would greet him politely, then retire to the far corner of the room until dinner was ready. The men were bound to talk shop, even during the meal, so Juliet would be spared the necessity of making idle and pointless conversation with a man who must, by now, consider her a useless nitwit.

Mr Wentworth rose politely as she made as unobtrusive an entrance as possible, then he and her father carried on their conversation, ignoring her completely.

Annoyed, but knowing she had no justification, Juliet sat on long squashy settee under the window, with her feet on the fur rug, and stared across the room at the fire. It had been a mild day with very little autumnal nip, and the fire was toned down accordingly. Only a thin, wispy column of smoke was visible.

The cook-cum-housekeeper-cum-everything else, Mrs Snowden, called them for dinner, and Juliet let the men go first. They did not, in any case, seem to remember she was there.

It was what she wanted, surely? She hoped Mr Wentworth would ignore her, that she would not have to
indulge in small talk, pretend to be interested, so she
really had no cause for complaint. Perversely, she *did*
complain, inwardly. She wanted to be ignored, yet did
not. If only she was so beautiful and shapely that Brook
Wentworth could not help but notice her, had eyes for
no one else . . .

She smiled at the idea. She was going to devote her life
to caring for the sick; men had no place in her scheme of
things.

'You are looking exceedingly pleased about something, Juliet,' her father observed, as they sat down.

Juliet smiled again. 'Just a passing thought, Father,'
she replied demurely, her fair lashes shielding her eyes
and her thoughts from him. If only he knew!

'I like you in blue. You have hair like your mother.
She always wore blue.' Dr Reed stared into space for a
moment, and Juliet pretended she hadn't heard his
complimentary remark.

Then Mr Wentworth put in: 'Nice safe colours, green,
or blue, as you say.'

Brook Wentworth's bland gaze met hers across the
table, and she struggled to hide the pain his remark had
caused. Evidently she should stick to nice, safe colours,
suitable for a nice, safe girl.

There was little conversation as they worked their way
through the delicious mushroom soup, then on to the
veal in a wine sauce. Mrs Snowden had excelled herself,
Juliet mused. She didn't care for alcohol in sauces but
knew her father did. And Mrs Snowden's one aim in life
was to please Dr Reed. She intended to be the second

Mrs Reed, Juliet was in no doubt about that.

And why not? Mrs Snowden was a widow, in her late forties, not a lot younger than her father. Dr Reed married late in life which was why Juliet had a father almost old enough to be her grandfather.

She didn't particularly care for Mrs Snowden, who was a bustling type of woman. She was excellent at cooking, cleaning—and organising. Juliet resented people who tried to organise her. Yet she loved her father and if Mrs Snowden could make him happy, she would wish them every happiness and, she supposed, would move into the Nurses' Home. It would not be fair to them to stay at Five Gables. They had the right to a bit of privacy.

'Oh! I beg your pardon?' Juliet became aware that Mr Wentworth had spoken to her, and she hadn't heard a word!

'I asked if you were settling down on Arndale,' Mr Wentworth repeated, stiffly.

The great man was displeased because she was ignoring him. Big-head, Juliet thought crossly, then realised to her horror that she'd spoken aloud. Two pairs of eyes gazed reproachfully at her, and her face flamed.

'I . . . I'm settling in, thank you,' Juliet said, quietly, her head bent over her meal. She didn't dare meet the surgeon's eyes, which would be dark and condemning.

'You seemed flustered this afternoon,' he put in, coldly, and Juliet began to hate him anew. Why did he have to mention that in front of her father?

'Last offices is hardly a suitable dinner-topic, Mr Wentworth!' Juliet flung at him, quite forgetting herself in her desire to hurt.

'Juliet!' Her father half-rose, but Mr Wentworth put a restraining hand on his arm.

Juliet was near to tears now but would not give the arrogant consultant the pleasure of seeing her weep.

'I nearly knocked Mr Wentworth down with the Last Offices trolley!' she snapped. 'It was my first death. Perhaps it shouldn't have affected me, but it did.' Her eyes appealed to her father for understanding, sympathy, but found none.

Dr Reed shook his head, irritably. 'Death is part of this medical business, my dear. It's just one of those things.' Clearly he was unable to understand Juliet's feelings and she felt more inadequate than ever.

Mr Wentworth said no more and the meal was ruined for Juliet, who merely pushed the lemon sponge around her plate, wishing their guest would suddenly remember he had an urgent appointment.

'Away home for the weekend?' her father enquired of Mr Wentworth, and Juliet shot him a guarded glance. Where was home? she wondered.

He nodded, sipping his wine appreciatively. 'I have a long weekend. Starts Thursday afternoon. Gemma is coming home on Friday.'

'Ah! *Is* she?' Dr Reed leaned forward, and Juliet almost did so as well. Gemma.

'Mm. Just for the weekend, though. She phoned me yesterday. Says she's looking forward to seeing the old place again.' Mr Wentworth caught Juliet's eye, and hastily she glanced down at the offending lemon sponge.

She began to eat the pudding, anxious not to appear to be listening. But listen she must. She intended to get to the bottom of the mystery.

'Will she be any better, do you think?' Dr Reed enquired, but the younger man merely shrugged, and the subject was dropped, much to Juliet's chagrin. Gemma was beginning to sound more like a wife than a sister. And the knowledge hurt. Could Brook Wentworth be married? It was a reasonable supposition. Consultants *were* usually married.

Juliet pushed her plate away. She didn't want him to be married. Like it or not, she was becoming fond of the man. He was arrogant, hateful, not at all the dedicated surgeon she would have imagined. What's more, he was utterly lacking in personality. A cold fish, that's what he was. Resolutely she put from her the memory of that brief interlude in the clinic. That had been a momentary lapse on the part of Mr Brook Wentworth. She knew it would not happen again. Whether married or not, he belonged to Sister Rosalind Paice, or to this Gemma, and was way beyond the reach of a mere student nurse.

CHAPTER THREE

As soon as she reasonably could, Juliet excused herself and fled to the sanctuary of her room.

Her bedroom was at the front of the house and from the big window she could look down on the drive and the minor road beyond. Five Gables was secluded without being isolated. It was only a four minutes walk from some local shops and on the outskirts of Garnhill. The house was big and rather ugly, Juliet admitted. A 'residence of character' was the phrase used by estate agents when describing such places.

Juliet's was the smallest bedroom of the five, with a narrow, sloping ceiling. There was barely room for her wardrobe fitment and single divan. The only other item of furniture was a hard chair. Her chest of drawers was in her father's room.

She stared unseeingly at the patch below, where Mr Wentworth's gold-coloured Rover was parked. She supposed that, if and when Mrs Snowden married her father, she would move out. If not, she would have to find room for all her belongings somehow in her own little den. She could not see the woman allowing her to flit to and fro when *she* became mistress of the house. She wondered what sort of house Mr Wentworth had. She knew he lived in a block of flats near the D.G.H. but seemingly he had a house tucked away somewhere. And Gemma was spending the weekend there, with him.

Savagely, Juliet thumped on the window-sill and hurt her hand. Bother Gemma!

Movement below caught her eye and she shrank back. Mr Wentworth was leaving. He certainly didn't hang about. Perhaps he wanted to call in on Sister Paice before bed. Or after bed, she thought waspishly.

She waited, listening for the sound of a car-engine, but heard nothing, not even the murmur of voices. Curiosity got the better of discretion, and, cautiously, she opened her side-window, letting in the October air.

She leaned out—to meet the equally curious gaze of the consultant, who glanced up at that moment. 'I was about to throw something at your window!' he hissed.

'Whatever for?' she gasped.

'To tell you I understood. About death being trauma-tic, I mean,' he called in a stage whisper. 'I *do* under-stand, Juliet.'

For a long moment neither spoke, and Juliet felt a lump in her throat. He *was* human, after all! He appreci-ated her distress, which was more than Father did. And he had waited to tell her.

Gratitude overcame all her other feelings for him and Juliet almost blew him a kiss. Just imagine how he would take that! She contented herself with smiling, hoping there was sufficient moonlight for him to see. 'Thank you, Mr . . . Mr Wentworth,' she called back.

'Why not come for a drive and thank me properly?'

'What? *What* did you say?' She raised her voice, and he put a finger to his lips.

'Shh! I've already said goodnight to your Daddy. You don't want him out here, do you?'

Weakly, she shook her head, then whispered that she

didn't. Nor do I want to come for a drive, she thought, but she could not find the right words to tell him.

Surprising herself, she shrugged into her fleecy-lined jacket, grabbed gloves and shoulder bag and hurried down.

She crept past her father's study where a chink of light showed under the door. She thought she heard the murmur of voices, and hoped it was Mrs Snowden.

Feeling greatly daring, she let herself out of the side-door, knowing that one of them would let her in the front-door later. She would say she had been for a walk, and would not be long, in any case.

The car was waiting in the road, and Juliet hurried out to it.

'Thought you had decided not to come!' Mr Wentworth smiled to take the sting from his words, and Juliet caught her breath. He had a beautiful smile. Why had she never noticed it before?

Perhaps because he generally scowls at me, she thought, tartly. I haven't seen him smile before, though I've heard him chuckle when he's been talking to Sister Paice.

Her expression became wary. What if Sister Paice found out about this pre-midnight escapade! A moon-light drive was innocent enough. It wasn't as if Mr Wentworth intended to make passionate love to her, but even so . . . A student nurse was dependent upon the goodwill of her ward sister, particularly when it came to a conduct report, and Juliet didn't want to get on the wrong side of her.

'Something the matter?' Mr Wentworth asked, setting the car into motion.

'Just wondering if I ought to tell Father,' she lied, not wanting to mention Sister Paice.

'You won't be out long. Shouldn't worry.'

She settled back, and wished she could enjoy the drive. It was a beautiful night, cloudless. She peered out of the car-window. Just visible was a startlingly clear crescent moon. The perfect night for a drive with the man you love, she mused fancifully. Except that she was a very junior nurse being taken for a short drive by a consultant. Nothing romantic in that!

But it could be, couldn't it? Suppose, just suppose, he stopped the car somewhere, by a lake, perhaps, and took her in his powerful arms, and . . .

Abruptly, she shut out the stupid daydream and risked a glance at Mr Wentworth. 'Are we going far, sir?'

Without taking his eyes from the road, he nodded. 'Ever so far, Juliet. Over the rainbow, if you like!'

She giggled, catching his infectious mood. 'Follow the Yellow Brick Road!' she ordered, and was rewarded by a husky laugh.

They drove in a companionable silence, until he turned the car off the road and into the parking lot in front of St Mary's flats.

Surprised, she was about to speak, but he forestalled her. 'I know. *Why* are we going to your flat, Mr Wentworth? I'm a good girl and never visit men at dead of night!'

Impishly, she smiled, then the smile died on her lips as the surgeon's dark eyes burned into hers.

Fire leapt within her, the first stirrings of desire. She wanted him to kiss her, and the disappointment when he did not was unbearable.

Shaken, and not fully understanding the emotion he aroused in her, Juliet allowed him to help her out of the car. Then he took her firmly by the hand and led her up to his flat.

St Mary's was a small block, on three floors, and Mr Wentworth had a front flat on the third floor. Still in a kind of daze, Juliet followed him into a small hall, then into a big room, sparsely furnished, which seemed to be living and dining room in one.

There was no settee, but two comfortable-looking reclining armchairs were stationed by the electric fire, and Juliet needed no urging to sit down. Her legs were going to give way any minute.

Mr Wentworth whistled a pop tune as he went through to the kitchen. Where, Juliet wondered, was the bedroom?

Then she beat her head with her fists, horrified at the turn her unruly thoughts were taking. He was a senior surgeon. He was simply being kind, bringing her to his home like this. Realising the day on the ward had distressed her, he was putting her at her ease, expressing his understanding. Nothing more. And the sooner she got that into her thick head the better!

'There. Coffee for two!' Placing the tray on the small, glass-topped table, he handed her a steaming cup of black coffee. 'Help yourself to milk and sugar.'

'No, thank you. Black is fine,' she said shyly, hardly believing that she was here, in his flat. What would Elma say? She sobered, dismissing the idea that she should tell Elma. No one must know.

Brook Wentworth settled back in the other reclining

chair, and yawned. He'd discarded his jacket and now wore what appeared to be a hand-knitted fairisle pullover. Did Gemma knit it? Juliet wondered, then felt his eyes on her.

'Admiring my pullover?'

She nodded, brightening. That might be a way to bring Gemma into the conversation. She simply *had* to know. 'Did your mother knit it? It doesn't look shopbought,' she added, then saw his face close up, his eyes harden.

'My mother? Did I have a mother? Consultants are much too old to have parents, Juliet!' he parried lightly, but his eyes remained cold, distant.

'You aren't old, are you?' she asked, momentarily sidetracked.

'Mm. Young for a consultant, I guess, but I shan't see thirty again.' He shot her a quick glance, as though expecting some reaction.

Juliet merely nodded. She'd guessed he was thirtyish. Not old exactly, but too old for her. The knowledge saddened her. They belonged in different worlds. It was as though he was a handsome Martian or Moonman she'd fallen for, knowing all the while that their interlude would be brief, that their love would never be consummated.

Love? Puzzled, she turned the word over and over in her mind. Surely she didn't *love* Mr Wentworth? It was a crazy idea!

'Cat got your tongue, Juliet?' His husky voice was sad, and Juliet hastened to reassure him.

'No, no! I . . . I'm just . . . I can't think of anything to say,' she admitted, feeling stupid.

That sexy chuckle broke from him, the one she'd heard coming from Sister's office, and she coloured. Swift tides of dull crimson suffused her throat, her cheeks. Her whole face burned and she wanted to die.

Immediately, he was contrite. 'Juliet! My poor little girl! I wasn't laughing at you!'

She didn't see him move because her lowered eyelashes were heavy with unshed tears, but she felt his arm about her shoulders, his fingers gently caressing her upper arm, his lips speaking low, soothing words.

Miraculously, the tears did not fall, but her eyes were sore with the effort she was making to control them. She would *not* cry!

He perched on the arm, half-sitting on the chair, half-lying on her, and her face was pressed to his chest— to the colourful pullover that Gemma had knitted for him. Realising that, she pulled away. He belonged to Gemma, or to Rosalind Paice, or both. Juliet didn't count; he was just being kind.

Remember that, she told herself sternly as she got up and stared at nothing in particular. 'Can we go back now?' she asked, in a small voice. 'My father will be cross if I come in late.'

'Look at me, Juliet.' His voice was soft now, seductive. Unwillingly, she turned her head, struggling to keep her expression neutral.

He rose, and stood much too near. Juliet wanted to push him away, to scurry down the nearest rabbit-hole, but was incapable of movement, incapable of making any rational decision. And when his lips claimed hers she shocked herself by responding avidly, as though she had waited all day for his kiss.

His mouth was gentle, his lips stroking hers, exploring the sweetness. She kept her eyes firmly closed, her mind devoid of all thought—except the knowledge that she loved this man.

The kiss went on forever, or so it seemed. Juliet's slender arms wound themselves around his neck, breathing in the warm, masculine, smell that was Brook Wentworth.

Abruptly, he disentangled himself, and stood, head bent, taking in deep gulps of air.

Juliet's eyes darkened with concern for him, and, greatly daring, she put her hand on his forearm, gently caressing it.

'No!' He pushed her hand away and moved nearer the kitchen door, not looking at her.

Angry with herself and with the surgeon, she stared at the electric fire, her cheeks flushed, her body still aroused, still wanting him. Oh, God! She had never felt like this before, never. Was it really love?

At a sound from the doorway, she glanced over, her expression veiled. He must never know.

Anguish shone out of the black pools that were his eyes. He was haggard and drawn, and she fought back the desire to fling herself into his arms, comfort him. She wanted, longed, to run her fingers through the overlong, jet-black hair, erase the dark circles from under his eyes, kiss away the worry lines . . .

'I'm sorry, Juliet. Very, very sorry. I'm getting into the Christmas spirit two months early!' he joked, but it was obviously an effort.

Realising his discomfiture, she played along with him. 'You aren't supposed to kiss the nurses unless there's mistletoe about!' she chided, with a bright smile fixed to her face. She was rewarded when the haunted look disappeared from his eyes, and he grinned at her, even white teeth gleaming.

'Sorry, Nurse! I'll try again in December—bring my own parasitic weed!'

They smiled at each other, uneasily. For Juliet the situation was still fraught with tension and she didn't know how to escape from it with dignity.

He sobered. 'I have too much respect for your father—and for you, to let things get out of hand, Juliet,' he said, quietly, and, numbly, she nodded. The time for laughter was over. It was serious, not something they could continue to joke about.

'How old are you?'

Frowning her surprise at the abrupt change of subject, Juliet muttered: 'I was nineteen last month.'

'Nineteen,' he echoed. 'Do you know something? With that Alice in Wonderland outfit, you look about twelve!

'Alice in Wonderland?' Perplexed, she gazed down at the blue shirtwaist dress, the plain, high-heeled court shoes.

'Not just the demure little dress, there's that white band holding back your hair.' He moved nearer.

'Oh! I'd forgotten that.' A velvet bandeau secured her thick wavy hair, forming a beautiful frame for her face.

Brook stretched out a hand and wrapped a few strands of her hair around his finger, giving it a slight tug before he let it go. 'Alice in Wonderland,' he murmured, while Juliet stood, perfectly still, silently willing him to kiss her again. She could not have him, he belonged to another.

She had no right to encroach on another girl's territory, but surely one more kiss wouldn't hurt? Just a small moment to carry with her always?

Her soft, young lips parted, and for a moment she thought her prayers were to be answered, that she was to be granted one more kiss, one final embrace.

He made no move to take her into his arms. Instead, he said: 'I'll never forget you, Alice in Wonderland. I'll bet you even believe in Santa Claus, and think that fairies are gauzy-winged creatures that live in toadstools at the bottom of the garden!'

Uncertainty darkened her eyes. Was he mocking? Yet she saw no mocking in the liquid depths of his eyes, only a strange sadness.

'There is no Santa Claus, Juliet,' he carried on, bitterly. 'And there is no scientific proof that fairies, gnomes, elves, etc, actually exist. One day, some young lad is going to take Alice in Wonderland down to the bottom of the garden and prove it. That will be the end of Wonderland—and the awakening of Alice,' he went on, half to himself. 'I just hope I'm not around when that happens, Juliet. I'd like to remember you as a soft, warm, unawakened child.'

Angry words of protest sprang to Juliet's lips, but the surgeon was already picking up her jacket and bag. 'Here. I'll take you home. You won't be very late.'

She had no chance to reply, to defend herself, to protest she *wasn't* a child. She knew the facts of life, she wasn't a fool. Even if she did look about twelve, she was nineteen. She was a woman, a woman in love.

In love with a man as out of my reach as the moon and stars, she reflected, knowing that arguing with him would be futile. Juniors didn't argue with consultants. Despite her feelings for him, Juliet couldn't forget the gap that separated them. He was too old, too far above her—and too heavily engaged elsewhere.

By the end of her first month on Arndale Juliet felt she had been a nurse for years. Everything began fitting into place. She was able to take an intelligent interest in each new condition she encountered, and her natural common-sense helped.

She did not, to her relief, commit the cardinal sin of offering fluids to a patient with a 'nil by mouth' sign on the bed. Elma almost did, but Staff Nurse prevented her in the nick of time. The patient, Miss Taylor, was one of Mr Wentworth's and if *he* had seen Elma . . .

Juliet shuddered at the thought. Mr Wentworth hadn't been to Five Gables since the night he'd kissed her. And, on the ward, his demeanour had changed. Whereas before he had been cold and distant, ignoring lesser beings whenever possible, now he became positively hateful, picking on staff for no reason that Juliet could see. She had been the innocent victim of his temper on several occasions, usually because she was running him down with a trolley, or talking to a patient when he appeared unexpectedly on the ward.

Mr Wentworth, Sister had pointed out gently, did not like a ward to look untidy. And young nurses standing around idly *were* untidy. When, diffidently, Juliet defended herself and told Sister Paice that patients were people and that nurses *ought* to talk to them, Sister's pale eyes had widened. The obedient Nurse Reed talking back was something new.

Juliet's feelings for Mr Wentworth were mixed. At times she thought she loved him, at others, she was positive that it was a stupid infatuation on her part. But, oh how she longed for just one kind word from him!

Juliet's even temper deserted her on occasions now, thanks to Mr Wentworth's niggardly complaints. Of course, she kept a firm rein on her temper when talking to patients, but the calm, biddable adolescent was growing up at last—and fast becoming disillusioned. Mr Wentworth, it was rumoured, would be leaving as soon as he found a post worthy of his talents.

He would probably go up to London, Juliet thought ruefully, as she stared blankly out of her window.

It was Saturday again, and on Monday she would celebrate five weeks on Arndale. After her tour of duty was finished she would go back to school for two weeks, then holiday. A holiday over Christmas, of all things! She ought not to grumble. Many nurses must envy her, those who had families and who resented being away from home at such a time. But Juliet knew her presence at home was preventing her father from enjoying a holiday in Switzerland. Mrs Snowden had fixed up to go with a friend, but the anonymous friend now found she could not go. The housekeeper wasted no time in offering to share the holiday with Dr Reed instead. Christmas in the mountains. A white Christmas!

Her father ought to go. He needed a break, even though he never admitted it. If she could fix up to work over Christmas . . .

The postman's tuneless whistling broke into her thoughts. She watched him crunch up the drive, heard the clatter of the letter-box, then idly watched him mount his bike and ride away. Eight-thirty already.

Without any real interest, she slipped quietly down the stairs. Most probably there would be bills, a few medical circulars. They had few relatives to write to them, and no close ones. Nothing of any interest . . .

Juliet's eyes widened as she stared at the strong, bold handwriting on the square envelope. Black ink on an expensive white envelope, the sort invitations were sent in. Brook Wentworth's handwriting. She ought to know, she'd seen it on enough case notes.

'Something exciting then, Juliet?' her father enquired mildly, putting a hand on her shoulder.

'Mm. This is from Mr Wentworth. Do you suppose he's inviting you to dinner?' She struggled to sound casual as she handed him the post, with Mr Wentworth's envelope on top.

'We shall have to see, shan't we?' To her chagrin, her father disappeared into his study, taking the letters with him.

It was unbearable. She *must* know! Yet she didn't want to appear too eager. She almost wrung her hands in her mental torment, then reason returned. Just suppose it *was* an invitation to dinner. That didn't necessarily mean that Juliet would be invited.

No, she agreed with herself, it did not. Mr Wentworth wouldn't want her there.

Juliet had to contain her curiosity until lunch. Not even over their mid-morning coffee did Dr Reed mention the invitation and Juliet couldn't bring herself to ask. Probably the letter wasn't important, anyway.

Lunch began with another of Mrs Snowden's home-made soups, too spicy for Juliet's delicate palate, but she got through it somehow. The housekeeper never joined them for meals, at least when Juliet was there. Today, though, she was dishing up their main course from the heated trolley when Dr Reed mentioned Mr Wentworth's letter.

'That letter *was* from Brook,' he said casually, then emitted a deep sigh of contentment as he saw the chicken curry. 'Ah! My favourite, Muriel.'

Mrs Snowden beamed. 'I know. You are a one for your curries, aren't you!'

She knew quite well that Juliet wasn't keen on curry, but that was a minor irritation. The letter drove all other thoughts from Juliet's mind.

'Was it an invitation, Father?'

'Yes. A dinner-party at Blair Place. I can bring a friend!' Dr Reed said, mischievously, and Juliet's eyes lit up, the sapphire-blue becoming more pronounced.

'Lovely! When do we go?'

There was an awkward pause, and her father and the housekeeper exchanged glances.

Juliet correctly interpreted the glance. He had already invited Mrs Snowden and she'd accepted. There would be no room for Juliet. Disappointment stabbed cruelly at her, but she tried hard not to show it.

'Oh! You're going, Mrs Snowden?' Juliet didn't need the housekeeper's curt nod. She already knew. 'You must tell me what his house is like. I'm eaten with curiosity!' She laughed, but it had a hollow ring to it.

'I didn't think you would want to go, Juliet,' her father put in. 'I imagined you saw enough of Brook on the ward.'

'Oh, yes, I do,' she assured him. 'I just wanted to see

his home. We all wonder what consultants' homes are like, even me!' she said lightly.

'If the youngster has set her heart on going, let her go,' Mrs Snowden said quietly.

'No, please!' Juliet protested, but could have hugged Mrs Snowden for her kind gesture. 'No, you must go, really! As Father says, I see enough of Mr Wentworth on my ward. He . . . he might be embarrassed having a junior to dinner,' Yes, he might. She hadn't considered that before. But, oh, she did want to see him again, to meet him socially. She wanted to meet Gemma, as well.

'No, I insist!' Mrs Snowden said, stiffly. 'You are Dr Reed's daughter, after all. It's only fitting you should go.' With back held ramrod-straight, Muriel Snowden marched out, leaving a wretched Juliet to meet Dr Reed's reproachful gaze.

'Why did you have to make such a fuss, Juliet? Muriel was looking forward to going. She was going to buy a new dress.'

'I didn't make a fuss! How was I to know you had already invited her?' Juliet cried, incensed at the unfairness of it all. If Mrs Snowden thought that Juliet was going to beg her to go now, she had another think coming. Having been grudgingly invited to Blair Place, Juliet was going to see the mysterious Gemma for herself!

The invitation was for dinner on the following Friday, and Juliet could hardly wait. Dr Reed reminded her to check that she wasn't on a late duty, hoping perhaps that he would be able to take Mrs Snowden after all. Juliet found that she *was* on late that day, but Sister Paice was agreeable to her swopping duties with Elma. If Sister knew why I want to change duties she wouldn't be so obliging! Juliet reflected, then began to wonder anew who would be there. A dinner-party. That meant about three or four couples, surely? There would be Mr Wentworth and, presumably, Gemma, plus her father and herself. Not enough for a dinner-party. He wouldn't invite Sister Paice as well, would he? No, not with Gemma there. Unless, of course, Gemma was away again . . .

By the time Friday came, Juliet's nerves were in a fine old state, and she half wished Mrs Snowden was going in her place. But that was cowardly. She had to go. She took extra care with her makeup, but deliberately kept it toned-down.

Some of her hard-earned salary went on a new dress, and she felt a twinge of remorse when she remembered that Mrs Snowden had been going to buy a new dress for the occasion.

Juliet's dress was apple-green. She chose green, remembering that Mr Wentworth had implied she ought to choose nice, safe colours. It was silky, the bodice square-cut but quite plain, the skirt softly pleated. She wondered afterwards whether a dinner-dress ought to be a dark, severe colour, probably black, but her father told her it was to be more of a buffet affair than a formal dinner, so the colour would do. She had inherited a few pieces of jewellery from her mother, nothing of any great value, but there was one rather nice triple gold chain and she decided to wear that, adding her own eighteenth birthday gold rose earrings.

Nervous and unsure of herself, Juliet nevertheless hid her unease successfully as she and her father drove to Mr

Wentworth's home. Blair Place, she discovered, was only a few miles away, tucked into a quiet cul-de-sac almost at the foot of the South Downs. It was about the same size as Five Gables but had a longer, tarmac drive, and an enclosed porch at the front.

Sounds of music and pleasant female laughter were evident as Juliet and her father got out of his old, but lovingly cared-for Jaguar. He patted the car affectionately as they left it and Juliet smiled to herself.

Mr Wentworth himself opened the heavy, studded door, the smile of welcome on his lean face fading when he saw Juliet.

'Glad you could come, Dr Reed,' he said, politely. 'Ah, you've brought young Juliet,' he went on, feigning surprise.

Juliet felt about twelve as his cool gaze swept over her. Young Juliet indeed!

'Juliet! What a pretty name. Are you still waiting for Romeo?' a girlish voice enquired, and a tall, slender brunette appeared behind Brook.

Juliet's heart sank. This lovely creature was Gemma? The fragile-looking girl nudged Mr Wentworth, urging him in a soft, well-modulated voice to introduce them. She was introduced as Gemma Wentworth, my sister-in-law, and Juliet's heart rose to its usual position. A sister-in-law! Then there must be a brother somewhere, Gemma's husband.

Meeting the other guests wasn't the ordeal Juliet feared, for the charming Gemma took a fancy to her and solicitously guided her around from guest to guest. Juliet had come prepared to dislike her, but that was impossible. Gemma was charming, utterly without guile or malice, and now that Juliet knew Gemma was married to Brook's brother, the whole thing took on a new aspect.

It was more of a party than a dinner, as her father had intimated. There were four other guests—a youngish couple whose name Juliet promptly forgot, and an older couple introduced as Dan and Margaret. Juliet later found out that both were doctors, Margaret being a psychiatrist.

Gemma took Juliet aside halfway through the evening and confided that it was her birthday. 'That's why this is a sort of party. I'm thirty today!' she giggled, and Juliet's mouth opened with shock.

'I thought you were about twenty-three or twenty-four,' she murmured. Thirty!

'Thank you, Juliet. You're a dear! Brook didn't want me to have a party. Said it wasn't advisable!' Gemma pouted, her hazel eyes taking on a faraway look.

'That must be because you've been ill,' Juliet said, rushing to Brook's defence. 'He doesn't want you to overtire yourself.'

Gemma laughed, a tinkly laugh that went on and on. She couldn't control herself, and was gasping for breath by the time she stopped.

Juliet, alarmed, tried banging her on the back, not really knowing what was best. Ought she to get Mr Wentworth?

But the tall surgeon was already bearing down on them, and gave Juliet a filthy look as though blaming her. 'Gemma! You'll die laughing one of these days!' His tone was amused, indulgent, and Juliet remembered his words when he'd visited them. 'She's young and lovely and I wish I wasn't so fond of her.'

He loved Gemma. That was plain for all to see as he bent over her. The laughter rapidly changed to tears, and Gemma couldn't control those either.

At last, Gemma lifted her lovely eyes to Brook and assured him she was all right, then she turned to Juliet: 'I'm never ill, my dear. Really. Isn't that right, Brook?'

'You are the picture of health tonight anyway,' he parried, his expression bleak and forbidding when it rested, briefly, on the blushing Juliet.

The look promised retribution at a later date, and Juliet knew she couldn't take much more. He adored Gemma and wholeheartedly disliked Juliet. There was no other interpretation she could put upon the evening's events.

CHAPTER FOUR

'NURSE Reed!'

Juliet momentarily closed her eyes. She would recognise that voice anywhere. Feigning surprise, she turned quickly. 'Yes, Mr Wentworth?'

The surgeon beckoned, and, conscious of curious eyes upon them, Juliet hurried forward. A hospital corridor wasn't the most private of places.

'I want to speak to you sometime, Nurse,' he began, severely. 'It's about my sister-in-law, Gemma.'

'Yes?' Juliet faltered. If he was going to grind her into the dust she wished he would get on with it.

'What time do you have lunch?'

'Lunch?' she echoed, then flinched as his eyes blazed down at her. 'I . . . I go about twelve-thirty, sir.'

'Until one-thirty?'

'Oh, no!' Strange man, thinking nurses got a whole hour for lunch! 'It's only forty minutes.'

'Forty minutes. Scarcely long enough for a first course, is it? Never mind, I'll find somewhere near. Be outside the main door at twelve-thirty. Precisely,' he added, in case she did not understand his instructions.

Without giving her time to tell him she had other plans for lunch, he walked briskly away. Numbly, she watched his tall, lean figure until he turned into the men's ward.

Equally numbly, she stared down at the form in her

hand. Now, where was she going? Her head cleared. Yes, the Path. Lab.

Trotting along to the laboratory, Juliet pondered over the consultant's words. If he was going to tick her off, he certainly wouldn't buy her a meal. Still, a free meal was always welcome to a student nurse. She must find time to tell Elma they could not have a Chinese takeaway after all.

Her errand completed, Juliet returned to Arndale, only to see another beckoning finger, this time Sister Paice's. Sighing, she hurried into the office where Sister was having a cup of coffee with two other sisters, and Staff Nurse Roberts.

Sister's gaze was flinty, her eyes definitely unfriendly, and Juliet went pale. 'I have just received a phone call, Nurse. From Mr Wentworth, no less. He has asked if you may have a whole hour for your lunch today.'

All eyes were upon Juliet, who shrugged and tried to appear unconcerned. She would *not* give them the satisfaction of seeing how upset she was. 'Very well, Sister. Thank you, Sister. I'm to come back at one-thirty then?' she queried.

Sister's shocked gaze rested on her. 'Yes, please, Nurse Reed. That will do,' she said sternly, and Juliet scurried out, hating Mr Wentworth more than she loved him. Sister Paice was *not* amused!

Juliet couldn't avoid hearing Sister Allen's scandalised comment: 'Wentworth surely can't be interested in *that* skinny little girl?'

Skinny little girl, indeed! Anger lent wings to her feet and she got through her remaining duties quicker than usual. Of course, he wasn't interested in plain little

Juliet. He certainly wasn't the Romeo Gemma had joked about.

Promptly at twelve-thirty Juliet made her way to the main glass-fronted doors. The sleek Rover was waiting, Mr Wentworth at the wheel, a forbidding expression on his face.

Heart sinking, Juliet got in beside him, after a moment's hesitation. Miserably, she wondered if she ought to sit in the back, but the surgeon made no comment and soon they were skirting Garnhill itself and driving along the main road.

If he doesn't find somewhere to eat soon it will be time to go back, Juliet thought, willing him to stop. A whole hour with Brook Wentworth! It ought to be wonderful. An hour all to themselves. She slanted a glance at his clean, sharp profile, then her eyes slid down to watch his long-fingered, capable hands on the wheel. She loved him. It must be love, mustn't it? His very nearness was awakening desires, needs, in her that she didn't know she possessed. Please don't be unkind! she said, silently. I couldn't bear it. It *would* be unbearable if he shouted at her.

She became aware that they were slowing, then finally stopping, in the car-park of a small restaurant. She wasn't sure where they were, but it couldn't be far from Garnhill. She would ask her father later.

Inside, soft pink lights glowed a welcome, and a bowing waiter took their coats, Juliet's being a navy hospital raincoat. She glanced self-consciously at her uniform. It was a plain white dress and she'd been careful to remove her belt, badge and fob-watch, but to her eyes her outfit still shrieked 'Nurse'.

Her appearance didn't appear to bother the surgeon, though, and she supposed he didn't really notice. Nervously, she fingered the bun into which she knotted her long hair whilst on duty.

The movement drew Mr Wentworth's attention to her, and he frowned. She placed her hands demurely in front of her as she pretended to study the menu. At least a frown proved he *had* noticed her.

'Well? We haven't much time. I got you an extended lunch-break as it was,' he said petulantly, and Juliet clenched her teeth, almost biting her tongue to stop herself from telling him what she thought of that!

'Yes. Thank you, sir,' she said, instead. 'I'll have the oxtail soup, followed by cheese omelette and french fries, please. There won't be time for pudding,' she added, eyeing him doubtfully. She wasn't sure he understood how important it was that she returned on time.

A glimmer of amusement crossed his face. At least, she believed it was amusement. 'That's what we shall have then.'

After the waiter had disappeared with their order, he fixed his dark gaze on Juliet: 'Gemma likes you.'

'What?' She turned startled blue eyes on him. 'Oh, your sister-in-law? I'm glad. She . . . she seems a fun person.'

He grimaced. 'Is that what you would call her? Yes,' he went on, consideringly. 'I suppose at times she *is* a fun person. She has a warm personality.'

I'll bet she has, Juliet thought, then waited, expecting to hear yet more praise of the attractive Gemma.

'She means a lot to me, Nurse.' The words came

haltingly, and Juliet was amazed to see the debonair surgeon actually blush. A dull red touched his cheeks, and he stared fixedly at the fork in his hand.

Juliet's eyes followed the movements of his long, sensitive fingers as he absently moved them across the fork, his thumb finally touching the tines one by one. She wondered, briefly, what those strong hands would feel like on her body . . .

Hastily, she shut out the tantalising thought, and was spared the need to comment, because the soup arrived just then.

Mr Wentworth explained to the waiter the need for haste, and the omelettes arrived just as they were finishing the delicious soup. It was just right for Juliet. The chef had been sparing in his use of herbs, unlike Mrs Snowden.

Without further conversation, the two of them tucked into their main course, and the meal was nearly over before the consultant again broached the subject of his sister-in-law.

'I want you to be a friend to Gemma,' he said, out of the blue, and Juliet nearly choked on a chip. She stared down at the almost-empty plate, hardly daring to raise her eyes to his. He would surely see the anguish in them. She *loved* him. Yet he was expecting her to be friends with the woman *he* loved! How could she stand it? It wasn't fair. It simply wasn't fair!

Carefully composing her expressive face, she looked up at last. 'You want me to visit Mrs Wentworth?' she asked, politely.

Mr Wentworth turned and signalled for coffee. 'If you haven't time for a pudding we can manage a quick cup of coffee, I'm sure.' He smiled at her, and Juliet's heart did somersaults. But he was switching on the charm simply because he wanted a favour. Remember that, Juliet, she told herself, firmly. It isn't because he enjoys smiling at you, because he doesn't.

'I realise I'm asking a lot, Nurse Reed,' he went on, still holding the smile. 'Student nurses don't get a lot of time to themselves. Then you have a lot of studying, but I did hope . . .'

His black eyes held hers, and she couldn't look away. She didn't want to, in any case. No matter what he asked of her, she would do it, just to please him.

'Gemma is easy to get on with, but . . .'

Juliet waited, wondering if there was a darker side to Gemma's nature.

'When she's well she lives at my home under the care of my housekeeper, Mrs Prentice. She's fairly young and she and Gemma get on well. I wouldn't ask you, but you made a hit with Gemma and she keeps on at me,' he went on, haltingly.

Oh, does she! Juliet thought.

'It isn't ideal, you being only a young girl, but your father says you are sensible and self-reliant.'

Juliet gasped. 'In the first place, I am not a young girl! You make me sound as if I've just left school!' she snapped, ignoring the ominous frown on Mr Wentworth's face. 'And in the second place, you needn't sound so . . . so patronising! I resent it!' she flared, miserably conscious that he would never smile at her again.

Brook Wentworth's wide mouth closed, firmly, as though he couldn't trust himself to speak, and they drank their coffee in silence.

Knowing he was too proud to broach the matter again, Juliet swallowed her own pride, and fixed her sapphire eyes on him, anxiously: 'When do you want me to call on Mrs Wentworth?'

He raised one of those fascinating bushy brows, then said, tightly: 'I thought you were turning down my request. Though heaven knows it is little enough to ask! The woman needs young happy companionship!'

As though ashamed of his outburst, he stared down at his cup, looking older and somehow deflated.

Juliet couldn't bear it. 'Please, don't look so sad!' impulsively, she placed her small, thin hand on the surgeon's arm, and they both glanced at it as though neither of them had ever seen her hand before.

He patted her hand, the warmth of his own hand sending little quivers of pleasure through Juliet. She knew it to be only a friendly gesture, a sign that he was pleased she was going to be company for his sister-in-law. Then a thought struck her.

'What about G . . . I mean, Mrs Wentworth's husband? Your brother?' She waited, keyed up.

'Brother?' He sounded dazed. 'Grant. He died two years ago. She's been worse since then.'

'Worse?' Juliet echoed. So, Gemma didn't have a husband now. And Mr Wentworth loved her.

He nodded, then rose, briskly. 'I'll tell you on the way back. You'll be late as it is.'

Juliet hurried out, the fear of punishment for being late no longer important. What mattered was hearing about Gemma's illness. Surely she wasn't dying?

'Is she dying?' Juliet blurted out, once they were back

in the warmth of the car, and the surgeon turned on her savagely.

'Of course she isn't! What a stupid question! I doubt that you are as sensible as your father said!'

Stung, Juliet mentally retreated. She had been slapped but didn't know why. Gemma *might* have been dying. How was she to know?

'I couldn't bear it if it killed Gemma,' he went on, as they halted at the traffic lights near the hospital. 'I'd do anything for her. Look, when are you off-duty?'

'Um. I . . . I haven't looked,' Juliet admitted. 'Not at the weekend, though.'

'Find out and give me a ring at the flat.' He scribbled on a piece of paper. 'Here. Let me know.'

He leaned across and released the passenger-door for her. In a daze she got out, then turned to wave, but the golden car was already on its way to the car-park. Evidently he couldn't wait to be rid of her irritating presence.

Miserably, she wandered back to Arndale, quite forgetting her brisk nurse's walk. He loved Gemma and Juliet loved him. The eternal triangle, for she supposed Gemma loved him as well. She would do all she could for Gemma, if by so doing she could please Brook Wentworth, the man she loved.

Friday. Juliet's day off, half of which she had promised to Gemma Wentworth. Mr Wentworth would collect her from home after lunch and take her to his sister-in-law.

Nervously, Juliet twined and intertwined her fingers. What was Gemma like, *really* like? Meeting her socially was one thing. Anyone could be pleasant for such a brief period, but now the mask might fall.

Brook Wentworth was casually dressed when he called for her. Evidently it was his day off, too. He was charming to her, and relaxed. Relaxed because he's hurrying back to the woman he loves, Juliet reflected, the bitterness rising up in her.

Why, oh, why, had she agreed to this? It would be impossible! Even if the surgeon was too blind to see, Gemma would notice. Juliet knew her face mirrored her thoughts. She couldn't help it.

'You were going to tell me about Mrs Wentworth's illness,' she ventured timidly, as he carefully reversed out of their short driveway.

'Yes. So I was,' he said, his good humour deserting him for a moment.

Just when Juliet thought he was going to ignore the question, he said, bitterly: 'She's an alcoholic.'

'Oh! But . . .'

'Yes?'

'But surely that isn't an illness?' she ventured. 'I thought it was a weakness of character and . . . and if they really wanted to reform they could. It's a question of will-power, isn't it?' she plunged on, only too well aware that she was rushing in where angels feared to tread.

Beyond a tightening of his mouth Mr Wentworth gave no indication that he had heard her, but, just before they reached his home, he turned the car into a layby and cut the engine.

Here it comes, she thought, despairingly. He's going to explode.

But he didn't explode. Indeed, he gazed sadly at Juliet, then, lazily, he trailed a finger down her cheek. She flinched, she couldn't help it. She could manage as long as he didn't touch her.

Abruptly, he put both hands on the steering-wheel.

'People turn to alcohol for a number of reasons, Juliet,' he said, quietly. 'Some of those who become alcoholic *are* weak characters. There is no use in denying it. Then those in certain occupations are more likely to catch the bug, if you can call it that. But lonely, depressed people can turn to the comfort to be found in a bottle of sherry, say. It doesn't necessarily mean they are weaker than the rest of us. It means they are seeking temporary respite from their problems, from their misery. Do you understand, Juliet?'

She nodded, not entirely convinced, but he had called her 'Juliet'! She would try to understand Gemma, for his sake.

'Gemma was very unhappy. Her marriage was a mistake from start to finish. Now, at the moment she is making an effort to kick the drinking habit. And I would be the happiest man in the world if she was finally cured.'

'I'll do what I can, but I haven't nursed alcoholics,' Juliet said quietly. 'Don't they usually go to psychiatric hospitals?'

'Yes. Gemma has been in one. She's also been to a special alcoholic unit. Plus general hospital. Plus long-time membership of Alcoholics Anonymous. She has tried, Juliet! This time I think we might make it.'

'I'll do what I can,' she assured him, smiling shyly. She longed to feel needed, didn't she? Well, here was her chance. A chance to be dedicated.

'Thank you, Juliet. To her amazement, he brushed her brow with his lips, then started the engine.

Juliet couldn't have spoken if the Queen herself had asked her a question. True, the kiss was only a friendly gesture, but . . .

She closed her eyes, tightly. There I go again. Reading more into the gesture than was actually intended. Get it through your thick head that he loves Gemma. He's just grateful to you because you're going to be friends with her. It's just *gratitude*, Juliet!

Oh, but if it wasn't? Suppose, just suppose, he was becoming fond of her, that her kindness and selfless dedication caused him to fall in love with her! He would have difficulty in choosing between Juliet and Gemma, wouldn't he?

Wishful thinking. Gemma would win hands down. Grow up, Juliet, she told herself angrily, as the car came to a halt outside Mr Wentworth's front door.

Before they were even out of the car, the door was flung open, and Gemma hurried out. A happy, laughing Gemma, her dark hair whipped about by the strong wind, her hands outstretched in greeting.

Flashing Juliet a brilliant smile, Gemma put her arms around Brook and hugged him. 'You brought her! You *are* good to me, darling!'

Juliet stood, miserable and embarrassed, her face flaming. Her heart was cold and heavy within her chest. If she'd needed proof of their love, here it was. All doubt vanished.

Swallowing her heartache, Juliet managed a weak smile for Gemma, who now hugged her.

'You must be cold, Juliet! I may call you Juliet, mayn't

I?' Without waiting for Juliet's diffident nod, Gemma
tucked her arm in Brook's and they all hurried into the
big warm house.

Come into my den, Juliet, while Brook does whatever he has to do,' Gemma said gaily, and Juliet followed her through the big, wood-panelled hall into a
small but cosy room where a coal fire threw out a cheerful
warmth.

She tried not to think about Brook, whose casually-
dressed figure had disappeared, but not until he had
given Gemma's arm one final squeeze. Juliet wished
desperately she was back at Five Gables. She couldn't be
a witness to their love affair. She couldn't stand it!

Something of her anguish must have shown in her eyes
and Gemma was quick to notice. 'Aren't you well,
Juliet?' she asked softly, appearing genuinely concerned. Juliet felt awful, begrudging as she did the other
woman's happiness. Why shouldn't Gemma be happy
with Brook? It was little enough to ask after the strain of
an unhappy marriage.

'I'm just tired, I suppose,' Juliet said lightly, going
forward to warm her hands at the fire. 'I shall soon be
leaving surgical and there's so much to take in before I
do.'

'Tell me about it. I did a bit of auxiliary nursing once,
just to see if I liked it, but I didn't!' Gemma confessed.
'All those bedpans!'

Juliet smiled. 'Auxiliaries do tend to get the more
menial jobs, I know, but on surgical we don't have so
much of the hard slog. I don't have any responsibilities
yet, of course,' she confided. 'I do quite a lot of odd jobs.
Or if there is nothing to do and Sister has a lot of

students, we can talk to the patients, or play Scrabble or Ludo with them.'

Gemma looked impressed. 'Imagine that! That's the sort of nursing I'd like! Nothing too dirty. Oh, you're back!'

Juliet turned as Brook entered the room, silently. He'd changed into slippers, fawn and black checked ones to match his pullover. Perhaps Gemma gave them to him, she thought, managing to avoid his eye.

'Tea is on its way. With home-made scones,' he said, smiling at Juliet. 'You'll like that.'

'Yes,' she said, politely. There it was again. Because he thought she was like a twelve-year-old, *of course* she would enjoy home-made scones!

'Brook,' Gemma put in, seeing Juliet's mutinous face, 'that was thoughtless. Juliet isn't a child being entertained to tea. She may not want a fattening scone.'

The surgeon's dark eyes swept over Juliet as though seeing her for the first time. 'She's very thin,' he mused.

'No! She's *slender*!' Gemma emphasised. 'She has a lovely slender figure.'

Juliet thought she would explode, but managed a diffident smile. 'Thank you, Mrs Wentworth. I don't need to diet, though. I can eat anything.'

'There you are, Gemma. Nurses eat like horses,' Mr Wentworth assured her, and Juliet wanted to run a knife through him.

She'd never felt like that before. She didn't recognise herself any more. The arrogant, thoughtless surgeon was stirring emotions in her she didn't know she possessed. Love and hate and . . . what more was there?

Fortunately for his continued good-health, Brook

Wentworth didn't linger once the tea had been drunk. Juliet felt more relaxed as his tall figure departed. She couldn't stand being near him for long.

'Brook has been a dear,' Gemma said, as she, too, watched the surgeon. She still stared at the door even after it closed behind him. 'I don't think I'd have survived if it hadn't been for him,' she confided. 'He's very uncomfortable about you coming, you know!' she giggled.

'Uncomfortable?' No more than I am, Juliet thought, resentfully.

'Him being a consultant and you being a junior nurse, you see,' Gemma explained. 'But I begged so hard that he had to relent. I even turned on the tears,' she confessed with a wink. 'Can you cry to order? It isn't difficult.'

'No. I . . . I've never tried.'

'You simply think of something very sad like a dog dying or your Grandfather being run over. That sort of thing,' Gemma went on, ingenuously. 'Or . . . or losing your baby,' she faltered, starting to weep, quietly.

Horrified, Juliet sprang up and went to comfort Gemma. 'Have a good cry. My mother always said there's nothing like a good cry. Does you the world of good,' she said, her arms about Gemma's thin shoulders. Sadness darkened her eyes at the thought of her mother. Juliet missed her still, sometimes waking up in the night, crying softly as Gemma was crying now. No one could take the place of a good mother. Heaven knows Mrs Snowden had tried, at the beginning, but was unsuccessful. Juliet had simply withdrawn further into her shell.

Perhaps Gemma didn't have a mother, either. She seemed to have no one but Brook. Juliet's earlier resentment and jealousy over Brook's love for his sister-in-law faded away to be replaced by a kind of motherly affection. All of a sudden she felt older, much older even than Gemma. She must be the strong one. Her own feelings, however painful, didn't matter.

When Gemma was more herself, she eagerly showed Juliet over the house. 'There's plenty of garden, plus an orchard. Do you ride?' she hurried on, and Juliet nodded.

'Not now, though. I used to as a child.'

'There's a riding school near the Downs, isn't there? We must ride together sometime. I haven't been on a horse for simply years, but I need fresh air and exercise, or so Brook says. We could walk on the Downs, too, couldn't we?' She gazed hesitantly at Juliet as though afraid of pressuring her too much.

'Of course we can, Gemma,' Juliet assured her. They had reached first name terms by now, and Juliet felt she'd known the older woman for years.

'You'll stay to dinner, won't you?'

'I . . .' Juliet hesitated, wanting to spend longer with her new friend yet dreading a whole meal spent in the surgeon's company. Lunch the previous week had been bad enough!

'No, I can see you don't want to stay! Does Brook get on your nerves?'

'No . . . yes, he does rather.' Juliet decided it was safer to be honest. Let Gemma think that was what upset her.

'He means well. He's ambitious, you know,' Gemma

confided, as they returned to the den. 'He intends to get on in the world.'

Juliet nodded. 'Yes, so I believe,' she said, politely. Ambition. Was that all that mattered?

Juliet was scanning Gemma's bookshelves when the surgeon reappeared. His dark hair was damp, as if from a shower, and his after-shave drifted across. Oh, Brook! she thought. What must I do to get you out of my mind? What *can* I do?

'I thought we might both take Juliet home,' he said, unaware of the turmoil he was causing Juliet.

Juliet's eyes darkened with pain. He didn't want to be alone with her, there was safety in numbers. 'I'll get my coat.' She hurried out to the big hallway and stood waiting for them, after she'd bundled herself up in her warm fawn suede jacket.

Moments later, an angry Brook Wentworth swept by, making for the stairs. Juliet's surprised gaze followed him. Surely he and Gemma hadn't quarrelled?

A laughing Gemma beckoned from the doorway and, mystified, Juliet obeyed the summons. 'He's in a temper because I said I was too cold to go driving. He didn't want to take you home by himself! I think he's a bit afraid of you, Juliet!'

'Afraid! How can he be?' Juliet spluttered. 'I never say a word out of place to him!'

Gemma smiled, then indicated that Brook was return-ing. 'Maybe you should!'

Thoroughly uncomfortable, and annoyed at being the innocent subject of the surgeon's anger, Juliet preceded him to the car.

In silence they drove to Five Gables. A cold, dark Five

Gables. Juliet remembered that her father and Mrs Snowden were going to the cinema. The housekeeper might not have left her an evening meal, assuming that she would dine with the Wentworths.

'Looks dark. Your father was going to lend me a textbook,' Brook Wentworth observed, as he courteously opened the car-door. He still appeared in a bad mood, but it was a controlled anger. She didn't think he would bite her head off, so she timidly suggested that he came in and help himself to the book.

'They are at the pictures. Father and Mrs Snowden, I mean,' she explained, diffidently.

'If you know where the book is, you could take it with you,' she offered. She didn't want to be alone with him, yet she did. She was reluctant to send him hurrying back to Gemma, though obviously he must be home in his thoughts anyway.

'Hm. Yes, I might as well.'

Juliet let herself into the darkened house. It was beginning to feel wintry, and she hurried to build up the fire in the sitting-room.

The logs had burned low but the room was warm and cosy, the firelight casting a glow over the splendid old furniture. It was homely. A real home in contrast to Mr Wentworth's house. That didn't feel homely at all. The furniture was good, in a modern style, the floors were thickly carpeted. Evidence of good taste was all around yet it lacked something. The woman's touch, perhaps. Gemma seemed not to be much of a homemaker. She told Juliet that she didn't like cooking and that the thought of washing dishes appalled her! They had a housekeeper who also did the cooking plus a daily so

Juliet supposed there was little that Gemma need do.

'There. That should keep us warm,' Juliet said softly, kneeling on the homemade rug in front of the fire. The last log she put on cracked, sending a shower of sparks out, and Juliet let out a cry, which she instantly stifled. She was being childish but it wasn't her fault her nerves were on edge.

'Are you all right?' Mr Wentworth stood by the door, making no move to comfort her, and perversely, Juliet was annoyed. Of course she didn't want him to touch her! Yet . . .

Sighing a little, she muttered that she was O.K. She replaced the guard firmly and went in search of the book Mr Wentworth had indicated.

Juliet had difficulty in tracking down the old-fashioned book and, staggering under its weight, she entered the sitting-room—to find Brook stretched out on the treble-sized settee under the window, fast asleep.

She crept nearer, anxious to observe him while she could. He muttered a name that she supposed was 'Gemma', then let one long arm drop. His face was handsome at rest, she decided, her heart aching. She longed to touch him, just his hand, perhaps, or brush his eyelids with her lips.

Juliet wondered what it would be like to kiss him, really kiss him. That evening at his flat when his lips had gently touched hers, that was almost her first kiss. She'd gone to a girls' school, and there had been no boys at secretarial college, either. Only on two occasions did she go out with a boy, and they were both friends of college girls. Both occasions were disastrous and Juliet had retreated after that. A few uncouth kisses pressed upon her trembling, unwilling mouth was not her idea of fun.

But Brook's kiss was different. It had excited, pleased her. Surely girls had as much right to expect pleasure as boys? Juliet knew she was naive but believed that, one day, true love would come. She would know that he was the one. Perhaps Brook was right. She *did* still believe in Santa Claus. Certainly it hadn't occurred to her that she would fall in love with a man at least eleven years her senior, a man moreover, who was loved by two other women. Hardly aware of what she was doing, Juliet moved nearer, as if drawn by an invisible thread.

Still moving quietly, she knelt by the settee, gazing at the dear, weary face of the man she loved. Shock kept her silent as those dark, velvety-black eyes opened and gazed back at her.

CHAPTER FIVE

'Oн! You're awake,' Juliet said inanely, only too conscious of the blush that swept over her face and neck. How he would laugh! That husky laugh she found so compelling.

But he did not. A tiny smile plucked at the corners of his wide, sensuous mouth as, lazily, he reached up for her.

Startled, but with no desire to escape, Juliet found herself half-lying on the settee, with Brook's strong, lean arms about her, his warm breath fanning her cheek.

Her heart started a rapid tattoo and he must have felt the loud, insistent beating as his arms tightened and she was pressed against his chest. With a sigh of contentment, Juliet laid her head on his shoulder and snuggled closer. This was heaven! Surely he did care for her, just a little?

Brook's lips brushed against her hair, then, tenderly, he nuzzled her cheek, his tongue gently exploring her ear. Juliet tried to control her excitement, the rising tide of desire. No one had told her that ears were so exciting!

'Please, stop it!' she squeaked, then heard that husky laugh.

'Why? I thought you were enjoying it!'

'I . . . I am,' she admitted, reluctantly, and he laughed again.

'Then why should I stop?'

'It's *because* I'm enjoying it that you have to stop!' Juliet said crossly. Surely it was obvious?

With a deep sigh, Brook released her and she found herself sitting on the rug. 'Stopping something we were both enjoying doesn't seem very logical to me, but it's just as well.' His voice was cold and distant, and Juliet swallowed her disappointment. Back to consultant and junior nurse again.

'I'm sorry that happened, Juliet. Think of it as a reward for being nice to Gemma.'

'Reward!' Juliet exploded, scrambling to her feet as the surgeon gazed up in amazement. She bit her lip until she drew blood. No, she couldn't say any more. He must never guess how she felt.

She tried to avoid looking at him, at the long, lean, masculine body stretched out on the settee. 'I don't want a reward for being friends with your sister-in-law, sir,' she said, coldly. 'I like her,' It was true. She *did* like Gemma and that made it all the harder.

'Good. I like her too.' He rose and stretched, and Juliet gazed fixedly at the fire after one brief glance at him. He was too much man for her. She was only Alice in Wonderland—wasn't that how he thought of her? Not as a woman at all. Why, he hadn't even noticed her slender shape until Gemma had drawn his attention to it. He didn't see her at all!

'You have a right to be cross, Juliet,' he said quietly, standing far too close for comfort.

'Cross?' she said, wearily. 'Am I cross?'

'I'll return Dr Reed's book next week.' With that he was gone. Juliet heard the front door close behind him. She was alone, unhappy and very cold. For a short while she had basked in the sunshine, a Caribbean holiday in the middle of an English winter. But only Gemma had the right to snuggle up to him, to rest her lovely head on his shoulder.

Juliet stared into the fire yet felt none of its warmth as, slowly, big tear-drops rolled down her cheeks.

'Guess what? I've given my first injection!' Elma's bright smile greeted Juliet on early duty.

'Did you? Was it very difficult?' The first injection was something Juliet had been dreading, but she knew Sister Paice expected all first-years to do at least one during their period on Arndale.

Elma made a face. 'It was scarey at first! We had it drummed into us—about how to avoid the nerve—but all the time you wonder. You know?'

Juliet did know. They had been taught in training school to draw a cross with their finger in the buttocks of the person who was to receive the injection. The point of the needle should be inserted in the exact centre of the cross so as not to hit a nerve and perhaps cause paralysis. But she knew it wasn't all straightforward. Sometimes people's nerves deviated from the normal and that was something the poor student nurse couldn't be expected to know. All she could do was inject where told to.

There was so much to remember, so many fiddly little details about nursing, and Juliet dreaded the mock exams they would have during their next study block. She tried so hard, was keen and willing, but couldn't remember everything she'd been taught. Nobody could. It was a question of trying to recall the important details and letting the rest take care of themselves.

To her horror, Juliet found that she had to give an injection that morning. Unfortunately, the patient was a very thin, bony lady, Mrs Salisbury. In addition to being thin she was also what Sister Paice called a 'professional complainer'—a person who, no matter how good the treatment, would find something to complain about at the end of her stay. And her complaints would be in writing, directed to the local newspaper as well as to the hospital administrator and anyone else she thought would be interested.

When Sister explained all this to her, Juliet was appalled. 'What sort of pleasure does she get from complaining, then? Surely she doesn't *want* us to make mistakes?'

Sister shrugged, clearly not bothered. 'Mrs Salisbury is one of our burdens, Nurse Reed. All hospitals and G.P.s have them. Their treatment was incorrect or their relative died because of a mistake by Nurse X. Or . . . Any one of a thousand things. I regard it as a sort of mental illness, Nurse, so that's how you must look upon Mrs Salisbury. More to be pitied than blamed.'

Quaking inwardly, Juliet accompanied Staff Nurse Roberts to Mrs Salisbury's bed. She tried to find pity for the patient in her heart, but it was extraordinarily difficult. No one *liked* Mrs Salisbury. There should never be an unpopular patient on a ward, Juliet knew. All should be treated alike, but, for heaven's sake, nurses are human! She fretted. Even tender-hearted Juliet couldn't like everybody.

Staff Nurse Roberts's manner didn't help matters. She was a proud, haughty girl who didn't seem to like teaching. Fortunately, Juliet had been well taught in training school about injection technique. In school, though, they stuck needles into oranges. On Arndale it was a different story—it was difficult to visualise Mrs Salisbury's bony posterior as a round, juicy orange!

'For goodness sake, Nurse! Do get on with it!' Mrs Salisbury had a loud, piercing voice, and although they were behind drawn curtains, Juliet knew all the other patients would drink in every word. And gossip about it afterwards to their relatives. *That* was how rumours started.

'Anyone would think you'd never given one before!' Mrs Salisbury grumbled, and Juliet swallowed nervously. If only she knew!

Staff Nurse was making jabbing motions with her right hand, a scowl on her face, but Juliet refused to be hurried. 'As a matter of fact, Mrs Salisbury,' she said, with a calmness she didn't feel, 'this *is* my first injection, so it's best not to rush it.'

There was a stunned silence, as Mrs Salisbury turned her head so she could see Juliet. 'Your *first* one!' she croaked, and Juliet nodded, then quickly pinched what little flesh there was and completed the injection, not without a sigh of relief.

Mrs Salisbury was too surprised to complain. Juliet had been expecting screams and cries of 'Murder, Murder!'

Under Staff Nurse's watchful eye, she made the patient comfortable again and, after breaking off the needle and covering the injection tray with a tissue, as she had been taught, Juliet trotted away, sending up a prayer of thankfulness.

She might have known she wouldn't get away that easily, for Sister Paice called her into the office later.

Juliet, quaking, walked in, to find Dr O'Boyle there too, his head deep in a textbook. He winked at her behind Sister's back, but Juliet pretended not to notice. It wouldn't do if Sister thought she was familiar with the medical staff. With one surgeon in particular!

'Nurse Reed, you had no business telling Mrs Salisbury it was your first injection this morning!' Sister came straight to the point, for which Juliet was grateful.

'It shocked her into silence, Sister,' Juliet replied demurely, and Sister raised her brows.

'True, but I bet even now she is composing a letter of complaint to the local rags. I can see the headlines—"Student Nurses used me for practice!"' Sister rolled her eyes, and Juliet's mouth twitched. It sounded funny, put like that.

'There is nothing to laugh at, Nurse!' Sister Paice snapped. 'It could mean the end of your nursing career. Though being a *consultant's* daughter does put you in a different league, of course.'

Juliet's temper rose. Sister made 'consultant's daughter' sound like it was something to be ashamed of. Over Sister's head she saw Michael O'Boyle shake his dark curly head warningly.

Perhaps he was right. There was no point in making a name for herself as someone who cheeked ward sisters. That sort of word soon got around. The hospital had an efficient grapevine.

'I'm very sorry, Sister,' Juliet said, still longing to give Sister Paice a piece of her mind. 'But I expect Mrs Salisbury was anxious, too. About the injection, I mean. It can't be nice having different people stick needles into your buttocks.' Juliet blundered on, feeling Dr

O'Boyle's interested gaze upon her face. 'I mean . . . that is, she must have been apprehensive.'

'Yes, I see. That will be all, Nurse.'

'Thank you, Sister.' Juliet trooped out, then heard quiet laughter coming from the office. Sister and Dr O'Boyle. They were laughing at her!

She liked Dr O'Boyle. How could he be so cruel? He was a beginner, once. Tears of shame sprang to her eyes and she hurried to the big linen cupboard—a favourite place for nurses to cry.

A few minutes later she emerged, a sadder and wiser girl. All her tears were spent. She did try, but if her best wasn't good enough there was no more she could offer.

Carefully, she removed her apron, washed her hands, and was about to pick up her cloak when Dr O'Boyle appeared, a smile crinkling the corners of his nice eyes.

She returned his smile without warmth then made a beeline for the hospital canteen. No way was she engaging in polite conversation with *him*!

'Nurse, dear! Wait!' His soft Irish voice drifted after her but Juliet pretended not to hear. She didn't want to speak to him any more. How could he be so cruel?

'Nurse Reed!' Juliet stopped suddenly. Those cold, autocratic tones didn't belong to Dr O'Boyle, they belonged to Mr Wentworth, another person she didn't want to talk to!

However, the voice of authority must be obeyed, so Juliet waited, impatiently, until the two doctors caught up with her.

'You wanted to speak to me, sir?' Juliet asked politely, but the consultant shook his head. 'Not particularly, but Dr O'Boyle was shouting at the top of his voice. Surely you aren't deaf, Nurse?'

Mr Wentworth's eyes were bleak and distant, his manner authoritarian, and Juliet's heart sank. Did he blame her for the interlude at her home?

'I'm sorry, sir. I was lost in thought,' she went on, coldly, turning her brilliant sapphire eyes on Dr O'Boyle. 'Was it something important, Doctor?'

Michael O'Boyle's grey eyes mocked hers. 'No, not really. It could keep until next Sunday.'

Mr Wentworth was already halfway along the corridor and Juliet sent a despairing look after him. Now he thought she was interested in Dr O'Boyle! Not that he cared, one way or the other.

'What happens next Sunday?' she asked, summoning a smile.

Michael O'Boyle grinned down at her. She hadn't realised how tall he actually was. He seemed a giant compared with her own five foot four. 'On Sunday,' he began, patiently, 'there is a sponsored walk. For a children's charity. And we are going.' Taking her firmly by the arm, he led her towards one of the many noticeboards.

Juliet knew she ought to read the notices but not being resident, she rarely did.

'There!' He thumped the board with a thick finger. 'Sponsored walk. That list underneath, Nurse dear, contains the names of people who intend walking. I have put my name down—now I'm about to put yours. Sister Paice told me you were due for a weekend off.'

Without asking her permission the young doctor wrote 'Juliet Reed' alongside his own name. 'That means you have to walk with me, my darling Juliet. I'll be your Romeo on Sunday.'

Juliet didn't know what to say. He was pleasant enough, but she couldn't forgive him for laughing at her. Then she read the names on the board. Could it possibly be that Brook Wentworth was walking, too?

It was too much to expect. He naturally spent his weekends with Gemma. No. She turned away, disappointment welling up. His name wasn't there, but Sister Paice's was. Oh, well. At least he wasn't spending the weekend with *her*.

'Does that enthusiastic sigh mean you're pleased, Nurse dear?' Dr O'Boyle enquired, laughter in his voice.

Juliet forced herself to smile up at him. It wasn't his fault his company was no substitute for Brook Wentworth's. 'Yes, I'd love to come with you, Doctor.' she murmured.

'Formal, aren't we? It's Michael with a capital M. Say it!' he added, teasingly, and Juliet obeyed.

'That's better. Can you be outside Woolworths at half-past twelve on Sun?'

Juliet could, and Michael O'Boyle went on his way. She wished he wouldn't always look so happy. In her present miserable state she didn't want anyone else to be *too* happy!

It poured all day Saturday and Juliet hoped it would do the same on Sunday, but it didn't. Sunday morning was cold and crisp and would be perfect for a long hike.

The atmosphere at home was a happy one during the weekend for Juliet had told her father she would be fully occupied over Christmas, that they were short-staffed on the nursing side and that she had agreed to take her holiday later. That meant, of course, that her father felt able to join Mrs Snowden in Switzerland.

Juliet felt awful lying to her father. He would have been hurt if he had known. But it was all in a good cause. The lie wouldn't hurt anyone and it meant he could have a really splendid Christmas break without worrying about his little Juliet. Mrs Snowden had actually hugged Juliet when she heard, so at least two people were happy. What she would do over Christmas, she wasn't at all sure. No doubt they would be glad of some voluntary help on the wards, particularly on the geriatric wards. Juliet was due there next, directly after her study block and the Christmas holiday. She looked forward to that. She would cheer the old ladies up over Christmas, the idea quite pleased her.

At twelve-thirty she stood shivering outside Woolworths, which faced the seafront. Several others were there, including Sister Paice who gave Juliet a cheery smile.

'Good exercise, Nurse Reed! Not that we poor nurses need any!'

Juliet smiled, impishly. 'I think we get enough walking in Arndale.' To her surprise she didn't get the snub she was expecting. It was unlike her to speak out like that. Idle conversation was for those who felt at ease in company. Perhaps the walk *was* a good idea, especially as it meant meeting colleagues socially.

Juliet was sad that Elma couldn't be there. She was on late duty, but that wasn't why she turned down the chance of fresh air and a brisk walk. To Juliet's horror,

Elma had confided that she might be pregnant!

'Guess I forgot the Pill one night,' she'd said laconically. 'You know how it is, Juliet.'

But Juliet didn't. She believed that a girl ought to wait until she was *sure* before committing herself to a sexual relationship. The first time ought to be with the boy you intended marrying. To Elma, sex was a way of life, she'd admitted as much. It seemed to have very little to do with love.

Love was what made the world go round. Juliet believed in love, but was that belief, too, part of her Alice in Wonderland existence? Was she, as Mr Wentworth himself suggested, living in a fool's paradise? Just waiting until some boy dragged her down the garden and gave her a practical demonstration of the facts of life?

'Ah, you're here, then!' Dr O'Boyle's big, capable hand squeezed Juliet's shoulder and she smiled weakly.

'Yes, I'm here, Dr . . . Michael.'

'That's better! Where is Big Chief then?' he went on, addressing Sister Paice.

She raised a brow in astonishment. 'You aren't telling me Mr *Wentworth* is coming?'

'The very same! Didn't I just tell you?'

'No, Michael, you did not,' Sister went on, frigidly, then beamed. Juliet turned to see what had caused Sister's change of attitude. Mr Wentworth and Gemma were just getting out of an old Escort, together with a couple of ward sisters.

Everyone was talking at once, but Juliet stood a little aside, feeling lost. Most of the others were senior, and older than her. She glanced at Gemma who hadn't yet seen her. Gemma was lightly made up, her skin and hair glowing with health. It was difficult to believe she became so depressed she had to drink. It was unbelievable that this frail, lovely woman needed any artificial aids to happiness. A thought struck Juliet and she wondered why she hadn't considered it before. Did Gemma drink because she didn't get enough attention from Brook? Did she care more for him than he did for her?

Just then Brook's eyes met Juliet's. He didn't smile, merely looked at—and through—her, then smiled down to Rosalind Paice. He had his two lady-friends. He didn't want Juliet there.

The knowledge hurt. He intended to ignore her. Juliet turned to look in Woolworth's window, then heard shrieks of laughter as three car-loads of nurses drew up. She knew several of them slightly, but they made no move to join Juliet or the senior set, presumably thinking that as a consultant's daughter she would not want to mix with juniors outside the ward.

If only they knew! Juliet was caught between two worlds and did not belong in either.

'Come on then, young Juliet! We're about to start.' Michael O'Boyle's voice soothed her hurt feelings and she gave him a brilliant smile, hoping he wouldn't notice that it didn't reach her eyes.

Unfortunately, Mr Wentworth chose that moment to notice Juliet, and his lips tightened ominously. Juliet didn't care, as she trustingly placed her hand in Michael's. The great consultant need not unbend any further. *She* was perfectly content with the company of Dr O'Boyle.

The crispness of the afternoon lasted another half-hour, then grey and purple clouds gathered slowly and some of the walkers lost their enthusiasm. All were sponsored for so much a mile, but Juliet didn't believe she would last even *one* mile. Fond though she was of fresh air, the wind was gusting in from the sea and her anorak wasn't as much protection as she'd thought.

Sister Paice, with Sister Allen and Staff Nurse Sellings, led the walk. Two doctors followed then came Michael and Juliet, with Mr Wentworth and Gemma right at the rear. Juliet couldn't see or hear them much of the time and her thoughts kept returning to Brook Wentworth. Had he come on the walk just to please Gemma? Was he warm enough? Might he not be too weary?

'Let's take a final breath of sea air before we head for the hills, Juliet!' Dr O'Boyle gently pulled her towards the railings, on the other side of which the sea hissed and growled, sending up white spray. An angry sea, Juliet mused. Cold and angry and dangerous. Like the expression on Mr Wentworth's face.

She leant over the railings, grateful for Dr O'Boyle's protective arm about her. Beside her another face appeared, and Juliet spun round sharply. It wasn't Brook, it was Gemma.

'Juliet! I didn't notice you! Brook, you didn't say Juliet was coming!' Gemma turned, big, reproachful eyes on Mr Wenthworth, who had materialised from nowhere.

He smiled down at the frail brunette, and Juliet hastily looked away. She didn't want to witness their moment of togetherness.

'We must take her back to the house for tea, Brook!'

Gemma cried, and Juliet flinched at the stormy expression on his face.

'No, no, really!' Juliet began, unhappily, then Michael O'Boyle saved the situation. 'Much as we would love your hospitality, Mrs Wentworth, Juliet and I might just creep away on our own!' He winked at Gemma, who shrieked with laughter.

Juliet wanted to die, yet it was for the best. Let Mr Wentworth believe what he wanted. He cared nothing for her, anyway.

They progressed along the esplanade, then turned down a side-street which would skirt the town and take them towards the downs.

Light rain was falling now, and Juliet huddled miserably inside the hooded anorak. She wore her thick, striped college scarf but it wouldn't be much use to her when it was soaked. A chill wasn't an auspicious end to her stint on Arndale! Six more days then she needn't see the arrogant Brook Wentworth again. Unless he intended she should visit his sister-in-law.

Pretending to take a last look at the sea, Juliet glanced back. Brook and Gemma were nowhere to be seen!

Disappointment stabbed her painfully. For a moment she faltered and only Michael O'Boyle's steadying arm prevented a fall.

'What is it, Juliet? Someone walk over your grave?' His tone was concerned and she smiled gratefully at him. He was rather a dear when he wasn't trying to be the life and soul of the ward. She wondered why she had never noticed his sterling qualities before.

'I was wishing it would stop raining.'

He chuckled. 'And there I've been wishing for a storm

ever since we set out!' he said, lightly, grey eyes dancing
at her.

Her eyes widened. 'Why? Are you so keen to get
back?'

'I thought it would give us an excuse to drift away—
together. I left my old car at the D.G.H. but we might
hitch a lift back. Then we could unwind over a hot cup of
coffee in the splendour of the canteen!'

They laughed, heads close together. Juliet almost
forgot the rain, which was getting heavier. Almost forgot, too, that the man she loved had slipped quietly
away, with the woman *he* loved.

But he hadn't slipped away and now his decidedly acid
voice broke in: 'Might I suggest we take cover somewhere?'

'Oh!' Relief swept over Juliet and she beamed at Mr
Wentworth. He hadn't deserted them!

Gemma's hazel eyes swept over Juliet's happy face
then onto Brook's. They narrowed, ever so slightly, but
Juliet recognised the signs. Gemma was jealous—something Juliet wouldn't have believed possible. No one
could be jealous of little Juliet Reed!

'I think sheltering is an excellent idea. Don't you,
Gemma?' Juliet said, hesitantly, turning on a smile for
Gemma.

'Yes . . . Yes, it is. I *am* rather cold,' Gemma confessed, her expression back to its usual blandness. Then she
swayed slightly and would have fallen if Dr O'Boyle
hadn't caught her.

He swept her up in his arms as though she were a
featherweight, and Mr Wentworth led the way to the
limited shelter of a doorway. He did not seem unduly

concerned about his lady-love's fainting fit and Juliet considered him heartless. Why, Gemma might be really ill!

Gemma was, by now, coming round, and bestowed a weak smile upon Michael O'Boyle who stared at the lovely creature as though captivated. Juliet wanted to laugh at the expression on his face, and had to turn away.

'Don't let it get you down, Juliet,' Mr Wentworth said, softly, as he passed her.

'What?' But he was already taking Gemma's pulse and gently scolding her for exerting herself.

What was it that mustn't get her down? Juliet wondered, then shrugged. Gemma was enjoying the attention of the two men. She wondered, briefly, if Gemma collected men like sherry bottles and threw them away with the empties!

Watching Gemma clutch pathetically at Michael's sleeve, Juliet began to think she was right.

CHAPTER SIX

WHEN the rain eventually petered out, the walk re-grouped under the direction of the radiologist. Juliet, shaking with cold, made to join them, but Brook Went-worth stopped her.

'No, Juliet. You're heading for a chill. I saw you shiver several times.'

Juliet brightened, her misery slipping away. He'd noticed? 'I'm all right,' she assured him. 'I wish I'd worn a thicker jacket, though.'

Brook nodded curtly. His own jacket was sheepskin and he didn't look the slightest bit cold, but Juliet refused the loan of his jacket, anyway.

Juliet looked around for Michael, then saw him with his head bent solicitously towards Gemma as she made some point.

'Shouldn't worry. Lover-boy will be back when Gem-ma's tired of him,' Brook said abruptly, and Juliet turned to him, eyes wide with astonishment.

'He isn't my lover-boy!' she protested, but the consul-tant seemed not to believe her.

'I would be surprised if young O'Boyle hasn't told Alice in Wonderland the facts of life yet!' he growled, and Juliet's temper flared.

He was unreasonable and pig-headed. Anyone would think he was jealous! 'Perhaps Alice already knows the facts of life, Mr Wentworth,' she said stonily, her head flung back defiantly. 'Girls start on the Pill young these days, you know!' Leaving him to make what he could of that remark, Juliet slowly edged her way back to Michael O'Boyle, Gemma now being deep in conversation with one of the other housemen.

Forlornly, Juliet gazed after the walkers, and heard their laughter even after they had disappeared round Fry's corner. She didn't know what had happened to the loyal band of supporters who were supposed to be cheering them on. Perhaps the cold had got to their bones, too. Now, only the consultant and Gemma remained, besides herself and Michael.

Juliet thought wistfully of the invigorating air on the downs and berated herself for not being better prepared. It hadn't looked like rain when she set out.

Michael went in search of a taxi, which were thin on the ground on Sundays, and Brook turned to Juliet: 'You and O'Boyle must come back to Blair Place to dry out.'

Juliet went pink, wanting desperately to accept the invitation, but knowing that he didn't want her there. She was almost certain Gemma didn't, either. 'I . . . I'll have to ask Michael. He might have other plans,' she said, innocently, and Gemma's tinkling laugh broke out.

'He probably has! Wants to give you a nice rubdown in front of the fire, I expect!'

Juliet gasped, then hurriedly averted her face. What a thing to say! She waited for Mr Wentworth to comment but he did not. Perhaps he thought that *was* what Michael had in mind, remembering Juliet's earlier remark about the Pill.

It was a foolish remark. Juliet could see that now.

Brook would believe she and Michael were lovers, that they couldn't wait to get away for a passionate session in front of the log fire at Five Gables!

'Don't look so disapproving, Brook!' Juliet heard Gemma say lightly.

Juliet busied herself wandering up and down the narrow road, looking in shop-windows. She didn't want to hear any more.

Michael O'Boyle, by some magic, found a taxi but, unlike Juliet, was pleased to be invited to Blair Place. He told the surgeon so, several times, much to Juliet's annoyance. He didn't need to fawn over Brook *quite* so much!

Blair Place was warm and cosy as the shivering group hurried in. Once the ironstudded front door was closed on the elements, Michael hovered uncertainly on the doormat. The house overawed him, and Juliet smiled to herself as the doctor nervously fingered the zip of his jacket.

'Don't stand there! *Do* come in!' Gemma made them feel welcome, or at least she put Michael O'Boyle at ease. Juliet wasn't at all sure *she* was welcome, though. A little frisson ran down her back. Gemma was not what she seemed to be on the surface.

Behind her, Brook spoke warningly: 'Try not to upset Gemma. She isn't well.' Then he was gone.

Angrily, Juliet watched his tall figure disappear through the middle-door. Apart from the fainting fit, Gemma appeared exceedingly well. Certainly fitter than Juliet felt! Shrugging, she followed Michael into Gemma's den. Gemma was hanging onto his arm, making him laugh.

Juliet didn't mind. She just wanted to sit as near to the fire as possible and daydream about Brook. She might, if she was lucky, see his face in the pattern of the coals as they burned.

'You must both change!' Gemma cried, turning to Juliet. 'You'll catch your death, then Brook will blame me!' she went on, laughing.

'Surely not?' Michael frowned at the infamy of such a charge. 'I'm sure the chief wouldn't blame such a lovely lady!'

'He *is* sweet, isn't he?' Gemma trilled, winking at Juliet. Then she caught hold of Juliet's hand, dragging her away from the fire. 'Come on. A nice shower while your clothes dry out, followed by a hot toddy and crumpets by the fire!'

Juliet allowed herself to be led up the winding staircase. Brook would not want her to resist. He'd instructed her not to upset Gemma, and the way to upset Gemma was to deny her whatever it was she wanted, so . . . Anyway, she was eaten up with curiosity, longing to see more of Brook's home.

Gemma insisted Juliet choose something to wear from her bedroom, and Juliet wouldn't have been human if she had refused. Gemma's bedroom was fabulous. Perhaps not quite, Juliet corrected herself. It didn't have a huge, circular bed or gold-plated fittings and a real mink carpet and curtains, but it was far more splendid than anything she could have imagined. She thought Gemma's taste would run to laces and pretty silks, pink for preference. True, the curtains were a soft pink and the bedspread was silver lace, but the rest of the room was darker, more masculine, Juliet decided—as though

Gemma shared the room and bed with a man. With Brook?

The hurt was too great, and quickly Juliet shut out the idea, forcing herself not to look at the big bed as Gemma fussed around her.

'Here, wear this!' she announced, holding up a leopardskin-patterned short bathrobe.

Juliet laughed. 'I can't go downstairs in *that*, Gemma! I'd get some very funny remarks from Dr O'Boyle!'

'Some from Brook, too,' Gemma said, her heart-shaped face sad for a moment. 'He admires you.'

'Who? Not Mr Wentworth, surely?' *That* simply couldn't be true. Whatever feeling Mr Wentworth had for her it certainly wasn't admiration!

'Mm. He said so. He said once you'd grown up a bit you would be a responsible, capable nurse,' Gemma insisted, big hazel eyes fixed unwinkingly on Juliet, who blushed.

'I'd like to be a responsible, capable nurse,' she faltered, 'but I do daft things, you know.'

'We all do at times, especially me,' Gemma confided, her good humour restored. 'Brook says I have an impish sense of fun. Did he tell you?'

Juliet hesitated. 'He did say you were fond of a joke,' she admitted, and Gemma laughed.

'Life is one long laugh, Juliet. When you have been hurt as much as I have, you'll find that the only way out *is* to laugh! If I didn't enjoy a little joke sometimes I would die,' she finished, then busied herself finding something more suitable for her guest to wear.

Juliet felt the tears welling up behind her eyes. Poor Gemma. And to think she'd been jealous of the poor

woman! Juliet felt mean and hateful. Gemma had suffered, was still suffering, and they must all do what they
could to make her life easier.

'This will do. Won't it?' Gemma held out a pretty
green and gold kimono, and Juliet's eyes brightened.

'That's lovely, Gemma!' Gently, Juliet fingered the
soft silk, marvelling at the colours and design. 'Thank
you. I'll shower now, shall I?'

Gemma nodded, and ushered her through another
door leading off from the bedroom. It was a small but
well-equipped bathroom, with a shallow pink bath, and
a shower cubicle behind a pink plastic curtain.

'I'll fetch some warm towels. Carry on. Take as long as
you like,' Gemma instructed, and Juliet's hands itched
to try the shower. At home they still had old-fashioned
bathroom fitments, which did not include a shower. Her
father was happy with his plain white bathroom, Juliet
supposed, and it wouldn't occur to him that his daughter
might long for something fancier.

Gemma was as good as her word, and Juliet had just
stripped down to her underwear when there was a tap at
the door. 'Everything all right? Here we are—loads of
towels!' She thrust several pink towels into Juliet's arms
and hurried out.

Juliet finished undressing, put on the shower cap
Gemma had thoughtfully provided, then soaped herself.
Even the soap was pink and smelled delicious. Like a
summer garden, Juliet decided, feeling wicked at enjoying such luxury. This was heaven!

Clean and fresh from her shower, Juliet stepped out,
removed the shower cap, and began to rub her hair
vigorously. She would have liked to shampoo it but

would not use any of the jars on the shelf without Gemma's permission.

Her hair dry, she wrapped herself in the bath-sheet and padded into Gemma's bedroom in search of the robe.

Michael O'Boyle, also attired in a towel, spun around at her sudden entry and gazed, horrified, at her. His towel was strategically placed but was only small bath size, and Juliet fled to the safety of the bathroom, her face crimson. Thank heavens she was wearing a big towel at least!

But there was no lock on the door and she was powerless to prevent Michael from pushing it open.

'Go away! Please!' She spoke softly, anxious not to let Mr Wentworth hear the commotion and come to investigate.

'She *said* you were keen,' Michael said, a big grin on his face as he reached for the end of her bath-towel.

Juliet's eyes widened in fear. 'Who said? For heaven's sake, keep your hands off me!' She backed as far away from him as she could, but his eyes glittered, and it was obvious that sight of her had aroused him.

'Please!' Juliet raised her voice, no longer worried about Brook, anxious now that he *should* appear, and rescue her.

'Juliet, don't be shy!'

Was there to be no escape? Juliet opened her mouth to scream, just as Michael dragged the towel off.

'What the hell are you playing at?' Brook Wentworth's furious voice penetrated her fear-numbed brain and, trembling, she picked up her towel and cowered behind it, leaving Michael O'Boyle to face his chief's censure.

Brook's shocked gaze went from one to the other, and Juliet wanted to die.

Her eyes beseeched him to understand, to realise that she was not to blame, that it was all a stupid misunderstanding, but the consultant was too incensed to listen to the halting words of explanation Juliet began to offer.

'Good God, man!' he went on, turning to the red-faced O'Boyle. 'Can't you keep your hands off her for a little while?'

'But . . . but she said she was willing!' O'Boyle protested, and Juliet gasped.

'I said no such thing!' she ground out, half-choking on the tears she was trying to hold back. 'That's a wicked lie!'

'But . . .' Michael O'Boyle began.

'Never mind! I've seen enough!' Brook snapped. 'Go and play around in somebody else's bathroom!' He strode out, slamming the door behind him, leaving a frightened and angry Juliet with O'Boyle.

'I did *not* say I was willing!' she screeched.

'No! No, it was her! Mrs Wentworth—*she* said you were willing. Just needed a bit of encouragement,' Michael muttered, staring everywhere but at Juliet's body. 'I'll go and get dressed.' He fled, apparently more frightened now than Juliet, who wrapped the towel securely around her and waited for a decent interval before tapping on the door. She couldn't stay in the bathroom for ever.

O'Boyle grunted in reply as she peered around the door. He was fully dressed now and willingly tossed the kimono to her. She emerged moments later, outwardly composed, but her thoughts were in turmoil.

'Look—about Mrs Wentworth,' Michael began, awkwardly. 'He'll never believe she told me to waylay you. And if he doesn't believe it, he'll chalk up a black mark against me,' he went on, morosely.

Juliet's lips tightened. 'Don't be so selfish! There's a black mark against *me*, don't forget!'

Michael shrugged. 'It doesn't matter so much about you, Juliet. Be reasonable. Everyone knows student nurses are . . . well, you know.'

'Promiscuous?' she asked, wishing she dared throw Gemma's silver-backed hairbrush at him.

'Sort of. More fun-loving really.'

'Junior doctors have a reputation for being "fun-loving" as well. It doesn't mean they are. And I'm certainly not!'

'No, I didn't think so,' Michael agreed, soberly. 'He won't believe us.'

'We aren't going to tell him,' Juliet said, firmly, and he stared at her in amazement.

'We've got to say something!' he protested, but Juliet shook her head.

'No, we can't. Because of Gemma. She . . . she isn't well. She mustn't be upset. Gemma told me she liked a joke. Well, she's had her joke. And whatever we say, Mr Wentworth will believe *her*—and the evidence of his own eyes,' she finished tartly, and O'Boyle hung his head.

'I'm glad you feel ashamed. My clothes seem to have disappeared. Perhaps they're drying out somewhere,' she went on, not relishing the thought of appearing in front of Brook in the kimono.

'That woman must have a weird sense of humour,'

Michael grumbled as they reluctantly made their way down the winding staircase.

'Very weird,' Juliet agreed. She itched to shake Gemma until her brains fell out, but knew she must appear calm and untroubled, not let the woman see she'd scored a point off them.

It was going to be very, very hard.

Juliet was silent and withdrawn at dinner, but her father seemed too preoccupied to notice. The following day he was due to attend a medical conference in London and Juliet was glad he was too busy to realise how unhappy she was. The state of shock had persisted, even though the dreaded confrontation didn't take place. Brook Wentworth was nowhere in sight when she and Michael fearfully returned to Gemma's den. Nor was Gemma, but Juliet's clothes were lying on the back of a chair, dry and pressed.

She'd hurriedly changed while Michael waited outside. He had intended ringing for a taxi, but evidently Mr Wentworth had already done so, according to the young housekeeper, Mrs Prentice, who let them out.

Mrs Wentworth was, she said, rather poorly and was sorry she couldn't say goodbye to her guests. Juliet assumed she would be blamed for Gemma being 'rather poorly'. Retribution would come, the only question being *when*? Brook had told her not to upset Gemma, who had stage-managed the whole affair very nicely. Now Brook believed that Juliet and Michael were lovers, and that the sight of them together had made his sister-in-law ill, so poor Juliet knew she would be blamed on two scores, at the very least.

That night she dreamed of Michael. At least, she supposed it was him. A tall, dark-haired man was pursuing her. The faster she ran, the faster her pursuer ran, yet always keeping the same distance between them. Then, though it might have been part of a separate dream, the dark man caught her and his hot lips were pressed against hers. She was still struggling when she awoke. Her body was hot and damp, and her father was shaking her.

'Juliet! It's all right. Don't cry any more.' He held her gently as she tried to focus.

'Was I crying? I . . . I had a nightmare. Someone was chasing me,' she faltered. 'And I woke you?' She sat up, wearily pushing away a strand of damp hair.

Her father's eyes were sad. 'Yes, you did wake me. You were screaming the place down. Poor Muriel thought you were being murdered in your bed!'

Juliet saw that Muriel Snowden was hovering in the doorway. 'I'm sorry, Mrs Snowden. I had a nightmare.'

'So long as you're all right, dear. You haven't had one of those for years, have you?'

Juliet shook her head. 'Not . . . not since Mother died.'

Her father squeezed her arm, gently. 'Juliet—there's something I have to tell you.'

'Yes?' Uncertainly, Juliet waited. Surely he didn't know about the scene at Blair Place?

'You shouted a name when you were dreaming. Presumably the name of the man you dreamed was pursuing you.'

'Did I?' Juliet shivered, waiting for the inevitable questions, but all her father said was: 'You kept shouting "Brook". Goodnight, Juliet.'

Dr Reed closed the door quietly behind him, and Juliet buried her face in her hands. Brook. *He* was chasing her, *he* had kissed her passionately. She'd been dreaming of the man she loved—yet still had run from him. Perhaps it was an omen, telling her that she ought to run from Brook, that they could never find happiness together. Gemma would see to it that they didn't.

'Nurse! You, that copper-haired Nurse!' Mrs Salisbury's voice could not be ignored. Juliet glided over to Mrs Salisbury's corner bed, wondering why the woman wanted *her*, in particular.

Mrs Salisbury sat up, looking remarkably fit for a patient who insisted she was at death's door.

'Can I help you, Mrs Salisbury?' Juliet asked politely, hiding her heartache behind a calm, professional manner; something eight weeks on Arndale had taught her.

'I want you to know I shall tell everyone about your injection technique when I get out of . . . *this* place!' She waved a disparaging hand to encompass the hospital as well as the ward.

Juliet sighed, trying to put her fear at the back of her mind. She couldn't bear it if she had to discontinue her training. 'I'm very sorry . . .' she began, but was waved to silence.

'I want *everybody* to know,' Mrs Salisbury went on, ignoring the interruption, 'that I hardly noticed when you gave me my injection! You have a kind, gentle way with you—not like the rest of these people!' Mrs Salisbury almost spat as Staff Nurse Roberts appeared at the bedside.

'Did you hear that, Staff Nurse? This little girl is better at her job than all the rest of you put together!'

Juliet flinched, pleasure and pride at Mrs Salisbury's words fading fast. Just wait until Sister heard the patient's opinion of the rest of her staff!

'I'm sure we all do our best,' Staff Nurse said stiffly, glaring at Juliet. 'But as Nurse is the daughter of a consultant physician it may be that she has the edge on we poor, *ordinary* Nurses!' Her back straight, Staff Nurse hurried out. No doubt eager to report to Sister Paice, Juliet thought bitterly.

'A consultant physician, ah? Which one? I don't know any Dr Reed.'

'My father is just an ordinary doctor, Mrs Salisbury,' Juliet assured her. 'Someone has to be consultant, anyway.'

She didn't hear Mr Wentworth's soft footsteps, and spun round in fright when a husky voice spoke in her ear: 'Causing *more* trouble, Nurse?'

'No!' In her agitation, Juliet spoke more loudly than she'd intended, and several pairs of interested eyes were turned towards them.

'I was telling Nurse Reed she has a nice, gentle touch, and it's a pity more of the nurses aren't like her!' Mrs Salisbury spoke up, smugly.

'Yes, she has got a gentle touch, hasn't she,' Mr Wentworth agreed, bestowing a charming smile on the patient; only Juliet could see that the smile never reached his cold eyes.

The consultant chatted with Mrs Salisbury for a few

moments, while Juliet hovered uncertainly. It wasn't his round-day and she couldn't imagine why he had come to Arndale unless it was to see Sister, whose tall figure was bearing down on them.

As Sister approached, Juliet thankfully melted away, her mind in a whirl. At least her name wasn't going to be on the front page of the local paper! She was proud that Mrs Salisbury thought so highly of her work, but knew she would be blamed for the woman's outburst. That was something else she'd learned on Arndale—junior nurses got blamed for *everything*!

To Juliet's dismay, the surgeon hurried after her, leaving a startled Sister Paice with the patient.

'Nurse Reed!'

'Yes, sir?' Reluctantly, Juliet slowed her steps and waited by the door of the clinic. Since that awful Sunday she had managed to avoid him. Now, on her next to last day on the ward, she was trapped!

She forced herself to meet his eyes, flushing at the contempt she saw there.

Brook stood, with one hand resting casually on the work-surface. He was as immaculate as ever, his lean, hard body relaxed, his voice dangerously calm. 'I thought I knew you better, Juliet,' he began, and she flinched, trying to decide to which of her many crimes he was alluding.

'Yet I found you, in *my* home, with a man—and I called you Alice in Wonderland!' he went on, his voice and eyes reproaching her.

'No, it wasn't like that . . .' she began.

'There is nothing wrong with my eyesight, Juliet!' he snapped, still keeping his voice low. 'You had been, or were about to make love. Couldn't you have waited? Did you have to fling yourself at him in my house?' His dark eyes sparked fury at her, and she wanted him to know the truth. He mustn't hate her, he mustn't!

'Please! It wasn't what . . . what you thought! I didn't tell him I was willing! It was all a misunderstanding!'

'Some misunderstanding!' he said bitterly. 'Do you know what your escapade did to Gemma? She heard you, laughing and carrying on in the bathroom! It upset her so much that she got drunk! Or very nearly. I found her in time.' He punched one fist into the palm of the other hand, and Juliet knew he wanted to hit her instead.

'I've managed to keep her off alcohol since she came out of hospital, Juliet! Yet, one thoughtless act from you and she's at the bottle again! Do you know what you're doing to me, Juliet?' Brook moved nearer, but Juliet held her ground.

'Do you?' he repeated, eyes glittering, and Juliet shook her head.

'I'm sorry. About Gemma, I mean, but she couldn't have heard us. There wasn't anything to hear,' Juliet said, stonily.

'Oh! A quiet affair, was it?' he said, sarcastically.

'Please! It *wasn't* an affair! Can't I make you see? Are you so blind?' she faltered, wanting to scream, but unwilling to embarrass him.

'Are you telling me there was—and is—nothing going on between you and O'Boyle?' His voice was calmer now, as his dark eyes bored into her.

She nodded. 'Nothing at all. He's nice enough but I don't fancy him *that* much.'

'Are you saying that Gemma lied to me, then? That

the whole episode was one of her famed practical jokes?'

Juliet was silent for a moment. Ought she to tell him? One look at his dear, tormented face, and she made up her mind. Brook had suffered enough. She couldn't implicate Gemma. In the echoing silence, she shook her head.

'Are you certain, Juliet?' he went on, searchingly. 'It wasn't Gemma's doing?'

'I'm certain. Dr O'Boyle misunderstood some remark I made. That's all.' She forced herself to look at him but flinched from the misery in his eyes.

'You were teasing O'Boyle, floating around in a scrap of towel. Gemma wasn't to blame,' he said woodenly, as though trying to memorise the facts, then quietly walked off the ward.

Juliet stayed where he left her, staring at the spot where he had stood, trying to imprint his likeness on her memory.

Brook, Brook. Her lips moved but no sound came. Only her thoughts went winging after him.

CHAPTER SEVEN

THE kidney, Juliet decided, was a very complicated organ. Over-complicated. Surely a simpler method of secreting urine could have been found? It maintained the water and electrolyte balance as well, though, so perhaps it needed its complicated apparatus.

One thing was for sure, if she was picked on to draw a kidney on the blackboard she wouldn't be able to. Trying to draw one in her notebook was hard enough. Miserably, she gazed at her effort. They had been through all the systems of the body briefly during Introductory Block, but now they had to study each system in more detail.

Juliet's next ward, directly after Christmas, would be Westdean, female geriatric, and urinary infections were common in women, particularly among the elderly, as was hypertension. Students had to be sure they fully understood the anatomy of the kidney before going on to a study of its functions and malfunctions.

The Bowman's capsule Juliet had just drawn was rather pretty, she thought, resembling a rose rather than the capsule and associated glomerulus of the kidney, but the drawing was hardly likely to bring praise from Miss Stevens, the tutor!

Three weeks to Christmas, Juliet mused, her mind wandering again. She was next to the window, but all she could see was a patch of pale blue sky and one or two little clouds, high up. It was cold and bright outside and she longed to be out there, laughing with Brook as he made some joke. Or they might go for a long walk after school. That would be nice. Then on to Blair Place for hot toasted crumpets running with butter. She wrinkled her brow. Should they have strawberry or blackcurrant jam?

'Nurse Reed!'

Startled, Juliet gazed into the iron-grey eyes of Miss Stevens. She had iron-grey hair to match, as well, Juliet thought in surprise. Now why had she never noticed that before?

'Nurse Reed! Will you pay attention, please!'

Juliet gave the tutor a sad, sweet smile, and murmured, 'Yes, Miss.' Definitely strawberry jam. Her dear, darling Brook was fond of strawberry jam. She would have to make some more when the strawberry season came around again. But that wouldn't be for months and months. December now, and a long, hard winter ahead. Perhaps she and Brook might go skiing up in Scotland if there was enough snow . . .

Juliet became aware that Miss Stevens was standing right in front of her, and her heart skipped a beat. Her foolish daydreams, of a life with Brook that could never be, slipped away. Kidneys were what mattered here and now. Dreams were for off-duty.

All around her, Juliet heard stifled laughter as Miss Stevens insisted that she describe the function of the kidney cortex.

She couldn't think straight for a moment, then it all came flooding back, the hours spent laboriously learning anatomy and physiology. To Juliet's relief, Miss Stevens praised her description, and the muted laughter died away. Let them laugh, she didn't care. The man she loved hated and despised her, so what did a few derisory giggles from her colleagues matter?

Feeling an outcast, Juliet walked home after school. It was quite dark, but the route home was well-lit and it never occurred to Juliet she might ever be waylaid. She considered herself rather plain and ordinary. And, oh, those freckles!

Absently she rubbed the bridge of her small nose as if hoping to rub away the freckles. Gemma didn't have any. Her pale, translucent skin was blemish-free. She was beautiful, too, her hair like a dark cloud of gossamer woven by one of those fairies Brook said lived at the bottom of the garden.

Brook. Everything came back to him. Brook, a tender smile turning up the corners of his wide, sensuous mouth—only that smile was always for Gemma or Ros Paice, never for sad-eyed Juliet.

Some Romeo *he* turned out to be! He played Romeo to Sister Paice's Juliet not to Nurse Reed's.

Another black mark against him was Juliet's ward report from Sister Paice. Oh, it was adequate enough. The woman had been scrupulously fair, Juliet allowed that, but it was the way Sister had looked at her. It was the day Brook trapped her in the clinic, the day she'd lied about Gemma. Sister Paice couldn't have known what she and Brook were discussing and might have thought they were planning an outing together, or even a spicy weekend somewhere. No chance of *that*!

The report showed Juliet to be an average student in most subjects, though below average in giving adequate support for medical staff. It was Sister's comments at the bottom of the form that bothered Juliet. Something about Nurse Reed trying hard but not showing Staff Nurse potential. A suggestion that she might have to do the pupil-nurse training instead.

It wasn't fair. How could a student of only two months' standing expect to show Staff Nurse potential? She'd tried hard, that bit was true enough. She'd got on well with Mrs Salisbury, the trouble-maker, hadn't she? She hadn't done anything spectacularly wrong, had always been polite and kind to patients and visitors, tucked her heartache out of sight as far as possible. What more did they expect?

Tears were streaming down Juliet's cheeks as she opened the gates of Five Gables. Not even the sight of the old house cheered her. The windows were ablaze with lights, welcoming her home, and, wistfully, she gazed into the sitting-room window, where Mrs Snowden had not yet drawn the heavy curtains.

Only the lace curtains were between Juliet and the scene within—her father and Mrs Snowden holding hands and laughing in front of the log-fire.

'I'm pleased for you both,' she whispered into the night. They were happy, their cup was full and she *was* pleased for them. But their happiness served only to underline her own misery, heartache, loneliness. There was an ache in her heart as she let herself into the house.

Marks and Spencers was crowded next day as Juliet hurried round in her lunch-break. She was desperate for tights, and never seemed to have enough.

She paused in front of the thicker, coloured tights.

The beige lacy-patterned ones were rather attractive and would keep her legs warm off-duty. In school they were allowed to wear slacks if they wished, but Juliet thought a skirt looked more professional, so did most of the others. She would buy the beige tights. Why not buy two pairs while she was there, a whole new wardrobe if she wanted to?

She had to make-do on her small student nurse's salary but, unlike most of the others, she had no rent or food to pay for. Yes, she *would* have two pairs.

'Juliet!' An affected voice drawled in her ear just as she got out her purse. Her mind still half on dreams of a new outfit, Juliet turned—to meet the gaze of Sarah Lloyd, a girl she knew from her secretarial-college days.

'Fancy seeing you among the masses!' Sarah trilled, and Juliet managed a weak smile. She didn't like Sarah, but didn't exactly dislike her, either. It was more a case of distance lending enchantment to the view.

Sarah was tall and ash-blonde, with big teeth and carefully made-up green eyes. Not exactly pretty but certainly smart. Elegant, Juliet decided. Everything about Sarah was elegant and spoke of money. She was a couple of years older than Juliet.

'I'm sorry I can't stop to chat, Sarah,' Juliet said, trying to sound regretful, 'but we haven't a full hour for lunch and I'm due back at one-thirty.'

'Back? Back where? Oh, that dreadful hospital place? You did stick it, then?' Sarah sounded appalled, and Juliet suppressed a smile. No way could she see Sarah tripping around with bedpans!

Sarah was, it seemed, a highly confidential secretary now, and she couldn't see why Juliet had wasted a whole year's secretarial training just to be a nurse.

Juliet, itching to get away, explained for the umpteenth time that her father had insisted on the office course just in case she didn't get on with nursing, but that nursing had always been her first love and yes, she *was* enjoying her training.

Sarah raised an artificially-pencilled brow. 'Your hands will be *ruined*, Juliet! Anyway, I'm glad we've met. I'm one short for my party at the end of the week and you'll do nicely!'

Juliet bit back a sharp retort. She would do as a stop-gap, would she? 'I'm sorry,' she began, but Sarah wouldn't let her finish.

'You were always too *quiet*, Juliet! You missed out on such a lot, you know. *Do* come! There's lots of nice boys coming. Or you could spend the evening talking to my tiresome Aunt Ina, if you wished.'

Juliet paused, tempted. She did miss out on a lot, that was the truth. And now, what did the future hold for her? Without Brook, nothing mattered.

'I knew you'd come!' Sarah took Juliet's silence for assent, pressed into her hand a slip of paper on which she'd scribbled her address and telephone number, then drifted away in a cloud of musk perfume.

Juliet, slightly bewildered, pocketed the piece of paper, paid for her tights, then had to run most of the way back to the training school.

Yes, she *would* go to Sarah's party. It would be noisy and the guests would bore her with their idle, staccato chatter, but she had to get out of the rut sometime. Why not now?

Soon, she would move into the Nurses' Home. That

was definite, since yesterday evening, seeing Mrs Snowden and her father holding hands. True, neither of them said anything to her, there was nothing out-of-the-ordinary in their behaviour towards her or to each other, but Juliet felt that an announcement of their engagement was only a formality.

Sarah Lloyd's party was Friday night, and Juliet spent the rest of the week busily planning what to wear. It seemed ages since she'd been invited to a party. Sarah's friends would be older and more sophisticated than Juliet. Did that mean they would wear sleek black dresses and diamonds? she wondered.

Eventually, after spending all her spare time in Garnhill-on Sea's trendier shops, Juliet found the dress of her dreams. Ignoring Brook Wentworth's well-remembered remark about copper-heads wearing green or blue, Juliet chose scarlet, a skimpy but wildly expensive dress with a perfectly plain bodice cut low, and slender ribbon straps. With it she wore her treble gold chain. Her hair she left loose, without her alice-band!

Critically, she gazed back at her reflection in the bedroom mirror. Hardly sophisticated, even with makeup. And leaving her hair loose wasn't such a good idea. It made her appear young and gauche, she decided, as she hurriedly dressed her hair in the efficient bun she used on the ward. She didn't like the look of *that*, either, but it would have to do.

Wishing she was five years older and more mature, Juliet hurried out to the taxi, half-pausing before the study door. Then she heard Muriel Snowden's laughter, so, head held high, Juliet swept out. No one must guess the heartache behind her brilliant but brittle smile.

Sarah lived in the next village, though she had a flat in London where she worked. The house belonged to her Aunt Ina, Juliet recalled now. Sarah had no family who cared about her, her parents having divorced and re-married.

The house was small but important-looking and set well back from the road and Juliet hesitantly paid off the taxi, her ears aching from the cacophony of noise.

It was some party! Aunt Ina must be a long-suffering old lady.

Juliet hesitated outside the front-door, which was ajar. Should she go straight in, or ring the bell first? It all sounded so loud! There must be dozens of people there. Fright kept her feet from moving so she pressed the doorbell and waited, wishing she hadn't dismissed the taxi. She shouldn't have come. She didn't know anybody there, except for Sarah. She ought to have . . .

'Well, hello!' A chunky young man answered the bell and grasped hold of Juliet's wrist before she could flee.

'I'm Juliet,' she faltered, and he chuckled.

'No? Where's Romeo, then?' He peered out into the darkness and Juliet laughed, nervously. 'I left him at home!'

'Good! That's what I like to hear.' He pulled her indoors, closed the front door, and peered down at her in the dimly-lit hall.

'Hm. Not bad at all. A little nymph.' He peered more closely. 'Come into the bright lights and I'll examine you.' He put his arm around her slender waist, and Juliet had no option but to be brave and face the other guests.

'Juliet! You came!' Sarah spotted her at once, and Juliet felt better. She had been so afraid she would stand unnoticed by the door, be the proverbial wallflower.

Soon Juliet was drawn into the throng and introduced to so many people that her head ached with the effort of trying to remember names. One name she did remember was the man who had met her at the door. His name was Andy Skilton, he was twenty-four years of age and worked in a bank. He was also the owner of flaming red hair, though he tried to darken it, he admitted. Eventually, when a few drinks had mellowed him, he admitted sheepishly that he hadn't seen her very well when she arrived, because he was short-sighted!

'But what I *could* see, I admired,' he went on fervently, his blue-grey eyes on her soft mouth. 'Next time we meet, I'll wear my dashing executive-style specs and take a really long look at you!'

Juliet, on her third dry Martini, giggled. She felt light-headed. Indeed, her head began to float away and, idly, she waved it goodbye.

'I won't be seeing you again,' Juliet said, suddenly. Of course she wouldn't. This was another, much different world. She did not belong here.

'Oh, but you will, my Juliet,' Andy insisted, nibbling her ear gently.

His action recalled Brook to her addled mind, and she fancied she saw him over in a corner, dark eyes fixed on her accusingly. But it was an optical illusion. Struggling to focus, she saw that there *was* a dark man in the corner, but he did not resemble Brook.

She let out her breath in a deep sigh. For a moment she'd thought . . .

'Tell me what ails you, fair Juliet!'

Laughing, Juliet turned her face towards Andy—and

met his descending lips. The kiss was brief and pleasant enough. No more than that. No drums sounded, cymbals clashed. No bells rang in her ears, but that wasn't his fault. Perhaps because she was lightheaded, his kiss didn't make the impact she felt it ought to.

'Practice makes perfect,' she muttered and heard Andy laugh as if from afar.

'Juliet, dear.' Sarah's voice brought her down to earth with a bump.

She sounded disapproving. Did she fancy Andy?

Juliet tried to concentrate on Sarah's words as the other girl led her away. Cool air from the hall hit Juliet as they made their way upstairs.

'There *is* a cloakroom downstairs but this is more private,' Sarah said. Juliet nodded, beyond caring. She was quite sure she didn't want the bathroom, but if Sarah thought she did, so what? Anything to oblige.

It wasn't the bathroom, it was Sarah's bedroom, she supposed. A much bigger room than her own bedroom, it reflected Sarah's personality—cool, uncluttered and elegant.

'Very nice,' Juliet remarked, thinking that some comment was called for. Idly she ran her finger along the polished surface of the dressingtable, then inspected it to see if there was any dust. There wasn't.

'Juliet! Pay attention!' Sarah's voice was frigid and reminded Juliet of Miss Stevens.

She said, sadly: 'He's your boyfriend, is he? Andy, I mean. I'm dreadfully sorry, Sarah.' She hiccoughed gently.

'No! He is not! You don't think he's *my* type, do you?' Sarah looked horrified, and Juliet giggled.

'No, he's too dull for you.'

Mollified, Sarah agreed. 'But he *is* engaged. I saw him pawing you and I wanted to warn you. Just a friendly warning.'

'Oh, yes. Just a friendly warning,' Juliet agreed, wishing she believed her. 'I'll tell him what I think of him!' she went on, determinedly, but Sarah's red-taloned hand was preventing her from leaving.

'No! It will cause a scene and upset Aunt Ina,' Sarah insisted, and Juliet could see the sense of that. 'I've a better idea. You stay here and I'll call a taxi for you. Andy won't know where you've gone.'

Juliet nodded, feeling rather sick. So much for sophisticated parties! Weakly, she sank onto the bed, her hand gently smoothing the fur counterpane.

Sarah disappeared, closing the door firmly behind her, and Juliet stretched out full-length on the bed, feeling wicked at enjoying such luxury. It was so comfortable. Imagine that—a fur counterpane!

She couldn't have slept for long and was just starting to dream when a hand roughly shook her awake.

'Brook!' she said, sleepily, and the shaking increased. It was difficult to open her eyelids, but she did so when a male voice said: 'Juliet! For heaven's sake! I've been all over the blasted house!'

Juliet focussed on Andy's kind, worried face, and she managed a sweet smile. So sweet that he groaned and bent his head towards hers.

Without conscious thought, Juliet wound her arms around his neck, closed her eyes again and made-believe he was her darling Brook.

Andy was stretched out beside her, his mouth exploring hers when the door burst open and they met the horrified gaze of a grey-haired lady who must be Aunt Ina!

Andy's face went as red as his hair, but Juliet was too shocked to feel any other emotion. Numbly she gazed down at her beautiful party dress. One strap was pushed down, her zip was undone and her small breasts were visible.

Juliet struggled to sit up and busied herself tidying her dress, leaving Andy to deal with a disgusted middle-aged lady, whose shrill tones were giving Juliet a headache. Or perhaps it was the wine.

Her hair fell about her shoulders, and half-asleep, she searched the bed for the pins and bun-net she had been wearing.

Ah, there it was. The net was next to Andy's tie, on the chair beside the bed. In reaching over for it Juliet fell off the bed and landed in an awkward heap on the rug, just as Sarah came rushing in.

'My God! What have you been up to?'

Silly girl. It was obvious to Juliet what they had been up to. 'No! We haven't . . . I mean, nothing.' Wearily, Juliet's voice trailed off, and she turned anxious blue eyes on Andy.

'We weren't doing anything, were we?'

'If you can't remember, it certainly can't have been very exciting,' Sarah put in drily, but Andy silenced her with a look.

'No, Juliet. I was just kissing you, that's all.'

'All!' Aunt Ina's pale eyes almost stood out on stalks. They were very large eyes. Prominent.

'Do you suffer from thy . . . thyrotoxicosis?' Juliet

asked, knowledgeably, and the woman stalked out.

'Really, Juliet! You've behaved badly!' Sarah stormed. 'Anyway, your taxi's here. *That's* what I came up to tell you.' She turned accusing eyes on Andy. 'How did you know where Juliet was?'

'I searched and searched till I found her,' he replied stubbornly, and Sarah shrugged.

'You two had better go. Aunt Ina is *not* amused. And neither am I!' she flung at them, slamming the door behind her.

Juliet and Andy exchanged rueful glances. 'Here, let me,' Andy leaned forward, intending to zip her up, but Juliet squirmed away.

'Don't touch me! Sarah had every right to be disgusted! I . . . I've never done anything so dreadful before.' She began to cry, miserable tears that inched their way down her thin face.

'Juliet, Juliet! Don't, please.' Andy seemed at a loss and Juliet supposed it did not occur to him to offer her a clean hankie, the way they did in romantic stories. Perhaps he didn't have a clean hankie on him!

The idea struck Juliet as funny and she began to laugh, half-crying at the same time.

Andy shook her again, zipped her up despite her weak protests, then, taking her firmly by the hand, led her down to the waiting taxi.

They were home before Juliet realised it, but Andy wouldn't let her pay her share of the taxi.

'Get a good night's rest, Juliet. Will your parents be angry?'

Juliet, thinking of Father and Mrs Snowden snug in his study, shook her head. With a sigh of relief, Andy assured her that he would go in with her and explain if she thought it would help.

Juliet shook her head again, then wished she hadn't as someone took an axe and began to chop her head in two. 'I'll be fine,' she whispered. 'One thing's for sure—you won't forget little Juliet Reed in a hurry!' she quipped, then, evading his arms, she slid gently out onto the drive and sat staring around her.

'Juliet!' Andy was half out of the car before she managed to struggle to her feet.

'I'm fine, don't worry! Goodnight, Romeo!' she called, slowly making her way to the side-door which ought to be unlocked. It was. Removing her shoes, she began to climb the stairs. There was a light under the study door and, reluctantly, she retraced her steps. She must let them know she was back, then Mrs Snowden could lock up.

Still in stockinged feet, she tapped on the study-door and went in without pausing.

Her father and Mrs Snowden broke apart, guiltily, at her entrance, and Juliet's bemused gaze lingered on her father. Even his moustache looked embarrassed! She giggled, quietly, then couldn't stop.

'Juliet!' Dr Reed thundered, his bewildered gaze going from his daughter to his housekeeper, but Mrs Snowden shrugged, as if to indicate that Juliet was *his* problem, not hers.

'Juliet!' Her father began to shake her, and Juliet winced as the shaking set her headache off again.

'We're getting married next week.' Mrs Snowden's calm, prosaic tones sobered Juliet.

She turned her stricken gaze on her father. 'Is it true?'

'Yes, my dear, but I wouldn't have told you quite like that,' Dr Reed murmured.

'She had to know, Stafford,' his future wife put in reproachfully, but Juliet heard no more. Her feet moved of their own volition and she almost ran upstairs, not pausing till she was safely in her room, with the door locked.

Married next week! They couldn't get married just like that, could they? They must already have made their plans, arranged the ceremony, ordered flowers, a photographer, a honeymoon . . .

Of course, Switzerland would do for their honeymoon. Romantic Switzerland, with its bright days and fun-filled nights. A honeymoon with Brook . . .

She almost tore the dress from her back, and it lay, a scarlet splash of colour, on the plain, dark rug. She didn't intend wearing *that* again.

Without bothering even to brush her teeth or remove her makeup, Juliet lay on top of the bed and closed her eyes. No, she didn't mind her father remarrying. It was obvious he and Muriel Snowden were well suited, if one enjoyed being organised. It was just the suddenness of it all, the way the knowledge was sprung on her.

Eventually, she slept, feeling little and lost and very alone, just as she'd done when her mother died. She was even more alone now. She felt she had lost a father—and she'd lost Brook. It would have been better if their paths had never met or intertwined. With a permanently broken heart, how could she live?

*   *   *

Saturday night is the loneliest night of the week. Somewhere she'd heard or read those lines, and it was true, Juliet mused.

Somehow she had survived Saturday morning and afternoon, had even managed to congratulate her father and Mrs Snowden. Her headache vanished and she was once more the young and healthy Juliet Reed—fighting fit and raring to go. Only there was nowhere to go to on a Saturday night, at least not on her own. True, there was a disco in Garnhill, there was also the cinema, or a small but thriving all-year-round theatre.

She could wander around the town as long as she was home well before the pubs closed. Or . . . Or what? She couldn't phone Elma in the Nurses' Home because Elma was most likely out. *No one* stayed in on a Saturday night, except Juliet Reed.

Knowing she was simply feeling sorry for herself, Juliet decided on the cinema and went to search for the local paper. She was browsing around her father's study when she decided she would borrow one of his books instead. He was bound to have one on geriatric medicine.

The doorbell rang and Juliet considered a moment. Would she answer it? Was it likely to be anyone important? It was dark and bitterly cold out and she couldn't let anyone linger on the doorstep.

She opened the door a fraction, remembering to secure the chain just in case the caller was unwelcome. He was. It was Mr Wentworth!

'Oh! I'm afraid Father is out. Was it important?' she asked hesitantly, not liking the nasty gleam in Brook's eyes.

'I came to see you, Nurse Reed,' he said, heavily. 'Do you intend to leave me on the doorstep?' He tried to push the door, but the chain held.

'I'm alone. Father wouldn't want me to open the door to a strange man,' Juliet informed him, then backed away at the furious oath he let out.

'Nurse Reed! Will you let me in—or shall I come back with a chopper and demolish your father's door?'

Some devil made Juliet refuse him entry. He had made her suffer often enough. Let him have a taste of his own medicine!

Then he collapsed on the front step. Alarmed, Juliet slipped the chain and bent over his inert form, trying to recall the stages of first aid. Breathing, bleeding and consciousness. They were the three main headings, though he didn't seem to be bleeding. And his breathing had sounded perfectly all right when he was snarling at her.

He moved, just as doubt entered her mind, and she found herself in his arms, being carried into the sitting-room. Dimly, she heard the front door slam as he put his foot to it, then she began to struggle, simply because she knew she ought to. She was content enough where she was!

Brook almost threw her onto the settee under the window, then sat beside her, one leg and one arm pinning her effortlessly to the settee. 'Now will you listen!' he ground out, and she nodded, resentfully. He needn't think he was getting away with it that easily. He had no right frightening her like that, and she told him so.

'I apologise. Pretending to be a casualty when you're

not is very foolish, and I ought to know better,' he agreed. 'I like that.'

'I beg your pardon?' Juliet tried to sit up, but he wouldn't let her.

'Your tartan thingummy. I like it. Green suits you.'

'Oh, this!' The tartan thingummy was a green and black checked pinafore dress that she'd bought in Scotland the year before. 'It's a bit short. I've grown since last year.'

'Have you?' His eyes did an excellent job of undressing her, and she blushed furiously. Why did he always make her feel so gauche?

'I can't see where you've grown, Juliet. You're rather thin.' He sounded disapproving and Juliet could have hit him.

'I'm sorry I'm not a big-breasted blonde!' she retorted, and he chuckled.

'I'm sorry you're not, too. But I didn't come to talk about blondes.' He became serious, and Juliet eyed him uncertainly. Was he going to tick her off, again?

'Gemma. She's in hospital again, taking yet another cure.'

Juliet met his gaze, levelly. 'I'm sorry to hear that. I thought she was cured?'

'Cured? I doubt she will ever be that, Juliet.' Absently he ran his long fingers through his dark hair and Juliet longed to straighten it. He was tired. He must be. Gemma didn't help him at all by drowning her sorrows. If she genuinely cared for Brook she would try harder to kick the habit, try to make him happy. Only that way could she be happy herself.

Juliet's sympathy for Brook shone out of her eyes, and

he drew her to him. Even if it was only her sympathy he wanted, not her love, she would give it gladly.

'Juliet . . .' he began, then the doorbell rang.

'Expecting someone?' Brook asked, and she shook her head emphatically.

'No. Will you go?'

'Of course.' He rose and stretched, then gazed down at her trusting face. 'I came prepared to shout and rave at you, Juliet. You should put in for a tiger-tamer's post! I feel at peace now.'

Juliet's eyes shone at the unexpected praise. He *did* like her, after all! Might that liking turn to love one day? she mused, while he answered the door.

She heard voices and was almost sure one of them was her father's. Puzzled, she waited expectantly, then Brook returned, his face grim. With him was her father—and Andy Skilton.

CHAPTER EIGHT

'FOUND this young man ringing the bell,' Dr Reed said gruffly. 'Didn't you hear it, Juliet?' His gaze swept from her pale, set face to Brook Wentworth's angry one.

Andy Skilton looked from one to the other as well. Then he held out a hand. In his palm lay three hair-grips that Juliet used to secure her bun. 'I came to return these, Juliet. I found them in my pocket.'

Brook's expression made Juliet want to run and hide. It was obvious what he thought. 'An odd place to find hair-grips,' he commented coldly, and Andy's eyes flicked towards him, uncertainly.

Juliet's heart was in her mouth. If Andy should say he had found them on Sarah's bed, she felt sure her father and Brook would take turns in beating her! But he didn't, of course. The episode did not show him in a very good light. Hardly a knight in shining armour, taking advantage of a young, innocent and slightly tipsy girl.

'Er, yes. I suppose it is,' was all Andy said, but Juliet's sigh of relief was audible, and both Brook and Dr Reed stared suspiciously at her. Dr Reed broke the ensuing silence by introducing the two men, and to Juliet's bemused gaze it seemed they were squaring up for a fight. Andy was half a head shorter than Brook, but bigger-built. In a fight her money would be on Brook. His murderous temper would make up for what he lacked in weight! He was a dangerous animal—a tiger, he'd called himself. Andy was more of a tame dog. Capable of biting, no doubt, but not needing to be kept behind iron bars.

'Would you like some coffee, Andy? I was about to make some,' Juliet said coolly, her one wish to escape to the sanctuary of her room. The last thing she wanted was for the two men to stay, but both accepted, and Juliet hurried out to the kitchen. Mrs Snowden was, thankfully, visiting her sister and wouldn't be back till Sunday lunchtime, so the kitchen was Juliet's own for a change.

She enjoyed cooking, and baking, but rarely got the opportunity these days. To her surprise, Brook followed her into the kitchen, and she flashed him a wary smile, to which he responded by grasping her upper arms and shaking her.

'What was that boy doing with your hair-pins?' he rasped, giving her another shake for good measure.

'He . . . he *found* them! He said so!' She tried to escape his clutches, but he wouldn't let go.

'How did they come to be in his pocket?'

'He took them out of my hair, then, being a tidy, methodical person, he put them in his pocket. He just forgot to return them afterwards,' Juliet said coldly, wishing he wasn't quite so near.

'Afterwards! After what? Answer me, Juliet!' He pulled her closer, his face only inches from her own. She felt his hot breath on her cheek, and, nervously, she faltered: 'He kissed me. There's nothing wrong in that, is there?'

'No. There's nothing wrong in a few kisses,' he agreed. 'Was it like that?' His head covered the remaining distance and, eagerly, she lifted her mouth for his kiss. It was a gentle, tender kiss, the sort she'd had romantic dreams about, but it was over too quickly.

Because she was ashamed at her response, she tried to push him away. 'No! I . . . I have to put the milk on. It's only instant coffee, I'm . . .'

'Or was it like this?' he interrupted her involved explanation. 'This' was a demanding, passionate kiss that left her shaken and bewildered when at last he lifted his head. Her mouth hurt where he had savaged it, and she put a hand up to her bruised lips, her eyes wide and wondering, her breasts heaving with the emotion he'd aroused.

'I could drown in those sapphire seas,' he said, gently kissing her eyelids. 'Deep, sapphire-blue pools of loveliness.'

Amazed at such lyrical remarks, Juliet attempted to laugh, but it was a feeble attempt. 'Please let me go. Father will be wondering . . .'

'Only Father? What about Andy?' Although she was still pressed to his shoulder, she could feel his mental withdrawal. Surely he couldn't be *jealous* of Andy?

No, of course he couldn't be jealous. Juliet tried to be realistic. He was curious about her relationship with Andy. That was all.

'I met Andy at a party last night. He very kindly brought me home—in a taxi,' she hurried on. 'He's a friend of a girl I was at college with.'

'I see. He won't be coming back then?'

Absently, she ran her finger down the maroon stripe on his tie. 'I don't expect so.'

He moved away, and she felt cold without his warmth. 'I'll let you get on.'

'Yes. 1 . . .' But he'd gone.

Numbly, she went through the coffee-making routine then put the cups on the trolley and wheeled it in. Her father and Brook were over by the fire, seemingly deep in shop-talk, while Andy stood by the window, just staring at nothing.

'Here we are. Four coffees,' Juliet said brightly, aware of Andy's eyes on her, afraid that Brook's brutal kissing had left some visible mark. It had certainly left an invisible one. She would never be the same again!

She took their coffee over to the doctors then invited Andy to sit by her on the settee. She was careful to sit right in the corner, and placed the coffee-cups and a plate of biscuits between them so as not to antagonise Brook.

'Who is *he*?' Andy asked, quietly, but Juliet put her finger to her lips.

'He has very good hearing. Surgeons generally have,' she whispered back, and he nodded, a puzzled frown on his face.

'Is he a relation? I mean, he almost bit my head off and all I did was return your hair-grips.'

'I know, and I do appreciate it, but I want to forget the whole episode,' Juliet said firmly, and he nodded emphatically.

'So do I! Particularly the old girl's face when she found us on the bed!'

He had raised his voice a little, though seemed unaware of it, and out of the corner of her eye Juliet saw Brook's head shoot up. He definitely had good hearing!

Sick at heart, she closed her eyes, wishing that when

she re-opened them, all three would have left her in peace.

'Juliet!' Andy's voice was exasperated, and, reluctantly, she came back to earth. She shot a quick glance at the other men. They were still arguing some medical point by the sound of it, but Brook's eyes were upon her, and she shuddered. It wasn't an encouraging look and boded ill for their future relationship.

'What are you doing tonight?' Andy asked, his eyes earnest behind the library-framed spectacles.

'I did think about the cinema, but I decided to study instead.'

'I know how difficult it is, fitting in study periods when you're too tired or there's something good on the box,' Andy assured her. 'We have pretty stiff banking exams, too.'

'Yes, I suppose you do. Not like doctors, though. *That* training must be tough going.'

Andy shrugged. 'They're dedicated. That makes it easier.'

'Are they? Dedicated, I mean? I always thought so, but they seem as keen to get on in the rat-race as the rest of us,' Juliet said firmly, and he shot her a surprised glance.

'I didn't know doctors *were* in the rat-race. Surely they go around healing the sick and not bothering too much about climbing the ladder of success? They work terribly long hours in hospital, I know. What keeps them going if not dedication?' Andy leaned towards her, as if to emphasise the point he was making, and Juliet tried to squash herself even further into the corner but found she couldn't move any further back. Andy's knee was

brushing hers and they were both aware of the contact.
So, Juliet felt sure, was Brook Wentworth!

'Anyway. Enough talk of dedication—we'll go out
and paint the town red, Juliet,' Andy asserted. 'You can
wear that pretty dress you were wearing last night.'

Juliet hesitated, conscious of the sudden silence. 'I
don't think,' she began, then her father broke in, irritably.

'If you were responsible for Juliet's inebriated state
last night, she most certainly isn't going out with you
again!'

Juliet spun round, angrily. 'It wasn't Andy's fault! It
was my own. Andy rescued me from a nasty situation
and . . . and brought me home!'

Her father looked discomfited, but it was Brook who
asked quietly: 'I understood you were in bed with this
. . . man. That doesn't sound like a rescue to me!'

Andy went red, but didn't attempt to defend himself,
and that made Juliet angrier still. 'We were not *in* bed! I
was *on* the bed and rather tipsy and Andy phoned for a
taxi.'

'No, it was Sarah who phoned,' Andy put in, anxious
to keep the record straight, and Juliet glared at him.

'Juliet is only a youngster and if you can't treat her
properly, you can leave!' Dr Reed thundered and Juliet
quailed. Her father's temper was well-known and was
enough to make even registrars head for the nearest
rabbit-burrow! Poor Andy stood no chance, so Juliet
leapt to his defence. 'Andy has done nothing to reproach
himself for, and neither have I!' She bestowed a kind
smile on Andy. 'If you wait outside, I'll do a quick
change and we'll go out.'

He brightened, then shot a furtive glance at her father. 'Are you sure? You won't get shot at dawn, or anything?'

'No. I'll be all right. Have you got your car?' she asked, ignoring the others as they made their way to the front door.

He had, and Juliet's eyes widened in surprise. A Mercedes, no less. The light from the hallway shone on its bronze body. 'It's big, isn't it?' Juliet walked around it for a better look.

'Mm. Plenty of room in the back seat!' he laughed, and Juliet's eyes flicked towards him, anxiously.

'It's all right, pet. I promise to be good. I'm too frightened to be anything else with your Dad threatening me with violence, and that other fellow . . . He was *livid!*'

'Was he?' Juliet perked up. Fancy him caring that much. 'He's always bad-tempered. He's a consultant surgeon, you know.'

'Is he? I'd better watch my step then. Wouldn't want *his* knife poised above me!' Andy said, only half-joking, and Juliet silently agreed. He was right to be wary of Brook Wentworth.

Leaving Andy to sit in his car, Juliet hurried upstairs, washed, brushed her hair and, dressed once more in the scarlet chiffon, she rushed down again—to find Brook at the foot of the stairs.

'Are you sure you're safe with him, Juliet?' He sounded concerned, and Juliet hesitated. To be honest, she wasn't completely sure of Andy, but wasn't going to let Brook know.

'Yes, I'm sure. He's very respectable. Really,' she

went on, uncertain of the state of his temper, but the surgeon shrugged and let her pass.

Wistfully, she glanced back as she stood at the front-door, but Brook was nowhere in sight. And he hadn't even commented on her dress!

The evening was a success and Juliet was glad she'd gone out. They went first to a disco in Garnhill, but the flashing lights tired Juliet after less than an hour, so Andy obligingly took her on to a club he knew where the music and the dancing were more sophisticated.

To Juliet's dismay, Sarah Lloyd was there, but beyond a cool greeting, Sarah ignored her. Aunt Ina was, pre-sumably, still not placated. Juliet felt she ought to apologise, but really there was nothing to apologise for. All she'd done was get rather tiddly then fallen asleep on Sarah's bed. It wasn't Juliet's fault that Andy had found her there.

Andy held her close and she felt every muscle in his firm thighs as they danced. His hands were warm on her back, moulding her to his body, and she fidgeted, trying to put some distance between them. Then he buried his face in the soft fragrance of her hair, which she'd left loose. 'You're lovely, Juliet,' he muttered, thickly, and she panicked.

'Am I?' she murmured in reply, then held herself stiffly for the rest of the dance. She mustn't encourage him, not even inadvertently.

Back at their table, he pressed a glass into her hand. 'Drink this. It'll give you muscles like Mr Universe!' he laughed.

Warily, Juliet sipped the dark liquid, then nearly choked as its fiery heat went down.

'It's only cognac, Juliet. Brandy and ginger ale, actually. More ginger than brandy.'

Not too sure about that, Juliet declined to drink any more, and Andy said sulkily: 'Not worried about your irate papa, are you? He's got no right to treat you like a kid! Why don't you stand up for your rights?'

Juliet shrugged. 'I'm his only child. Fathers are naturally protective of their daughters, aren't they? He didn't mean to sound Victorian,' she defended her father.

But drink had made her companion belligerent. 'What about that other guy? The tall one who kept on about the bed.'

'Oh, Mr Wentworth,' Juliet said, distantly. 'He's an old friend of the family.'

'I think he had a damn cheek! Bet *he'd* like to get you on a bed!' Andy said, darkly.

'He's just concerned for me.' Juliet said. 'It's good to know someone *cares*. Probably he's waiting at home for my return, axe at the ready!' she joked, but Andy couldn't see the joke.

His good humour returned later on, and they chatted away like old friends on the way back. Juliet found they shared an interest in lighter, classical music. Andy liked the heavier items as well, and mentioned Wagner.

'I find his work too serious,' Juliet said, firmly. 'But I love the Flying Dutchman. It's so romantic.'

Andy hooted with laughter. '*That's* the only piece of Wagner I can't stand! Imagine that lovely girl throwing herself into the sea because of some old, bewhiskered phantom sailor!'

'That's what love is all about!' Juliet cried. 'She loved the Dutchman!'

'Don't talk to me about love! I've finished with it,' Andy retorted, then Juliet recalled Sarah's words: He's engaged.

She bit her lip, feeling mean and underhand because she had accepted an invitation from someone else's fiancé. 'I shouldn't have come. I forgot you were engaged.'

'*Were* is the correct word, Juliet. I broke it off a couple of weeks ago. Before I met you,' he added, and Juliet felt better. 'I told her she could keep the ring but she wasn't having me!'

Juliet waited, but Andy declined to say any more about his ex-fiancée, so she went on to describe some of the horrors of her study-block, and in no time at all they were back at Five Gables.

'Plenty of lights on,' Andy grunted. 'Father must be waiting up.'

'Oh, no. Not for me,' Juliet assured him. 'He always goes to bed late. Particularly weekends.'

'It's very late now,' Andy pointed out. 'Nearly one o'clock.'

'Is it? I had better slip in the side door and creep up to bed, then.'

She tensed, prepared for a passionate embrace, but Andy contented himself with giving her arm a squeeze then dropping a light kiss on her brow. 'See you Tuesday night, then?'

'Mm. Thank you for a lovely evening, Andy,' Juliet said, grateful that their goodbye wasn't to be a protracted one.

'Goodnight, sweetheart!' Andy called, in a stage whisper, and Juliet winced. Her father slept at the back of the house but he might just be up, waiting for her.

Not waiting to see Andy go, Juliet hurried in out of the cold. The mist which had been hanging around all day had come down now and it was chilly, a damp chilliness that went right through to her bones. She preferred it crisp, even snowy, rather than the penetrating dampness of the mist. It didn't seem Christmassy, more like October.

Methodically, she locked and bolted the doors, and went from room to room turning off lights. Father must be in bed and had left the lights on for her, something he or Mrs Snowden did when Juliet was on late duty. It was comforting. It must be awful coming home to a dark, empty house, Juliet mused, then realised that, over Christmas, that was exactly what she would be doing, for the others would be away.

She shivered as she wearily climbed the stairs. She would be even more lonely than usual. Was Brook going away for Christmas? she wondered. Presumably Gemma would still be in hospital.

She glanced down at the vivid dress. Brook hadn't even noticed. She might have been wearing a sack for all the interest he took! He did like her tartan pinafore dress, though, and she resolved to wear it tomorrow, even though he would not see it. Of course, it wouldn't be tomorrow. Tomorrow was today! Sunday morning.

There wasn't a light under her father's door, so she crept into the bathroom, deciding to have a hot bath to get some of the stiffness out of her joints. It wasn't often she danced, and she'd rather overdone it.

She found herself drifting off to sleep in the bath, and shook herself awake. The water was barely warm now.

Surely she hadn't dozed?

Groggily, she stood up, then the door opened and Brook Wentworth stood there, eyebrows raised. Stark naked and barely awake, she stared at him, too tired to be embarrassed. Then realisation dawned, and she belatedly reached for the bath-towel, holding it in front of her defensively.

'Well, well!' Brook exclaimed, laughter in his voice. 'Lady Godiva without the horse!'

'Go away!' she hissed, anger over-riding her embarrassment, but he didn't attempt to move. He had on only a gold silky bathrobe that she recognised as one she'd bought her father, and it reached only to Brook's knees. He looked very sexy standing by the door.

Ashamed of her erotic thoughts, Juliet took refuge in temper. 'Get out! I hate the sight of you!' She struggled to keep her voice low, fearing to wake her father and cause a scene, but she would have to if that terrible man didn't go.

'I *have* seen naked young ladies before, Juliet,' Brook commented gently, not taking his eyes off her flushed face.

'Yes, on your theatre table! Not . . . not in a bathroom!'

'On the contrary, there's nothing quite as enjoyable as sharing a bath with a woman!' He moved nearer, and she began to shake, as though with a chill. To say she was frightened was an understatement. She was terrified! Not only of what he might do, but of her own reaction to it. He must never know she wanted, coveted, desired and loved him. He mustn't!

'I was only teasing, Juliet,' Brook assured her, gently.

'Oh!' Disappointment shot through her, but she pretended it was relief. 'Please go, then.'

With a sigh, he furned.

'No! Wait . . .' she begged, and he raised a bushy brow.

'You want something, Juliet? Your back scrubbed?'

'No!' In her indignation, she dropped the towel, which she'd been clutching tightly all the while. Her horrified gaze followed the towel as it plopped into the bathwater, and she wanted to cry. Never had she felt so humiliated, not even when Sarah's Aunt Ina had found her on the bed with Andy. Brook would assume she'd dropped it deliberately.

'Here, take this. I'll bring out a bigger one.' Brook thrust a hand-towel into her hands, and she gazed uncomprehendingly at it.

'For God's sake, Juliet! Wrap it around you!' Brook was back, with an armful of towels he must have raked out of the airing-cupboard, and he flung a gaudy beach-towel at her. 'You'll get your death, girl! Let me.' Deftly, he wrapped the big towel around her, skirt-style, then draped the smaller towel around her shoulders. It just covered her breasts.

'Come on! Out of that bath!' he commanded, and Juliet was lifted out, held against him for a brief, precious second, then carried through to her bedroom. Brook's bare feet made no sound on the thick carpet, and Juliet felt she was floating through the air. Only his arms were real, and the animal warmth of his body through the bath-robe.

Wearily she closed her eyes and nestled against him. She was safe and secure there, in his arms. It felt so *right*, as though she had always belonged there.

Gemma belongs in his arms. The words ran through Juliet's head, and she made a small sound of protest as Brook gently laid her on her divan.

'There. Get dried quickly, then into bed, Juliet. Need anything else?' He leaned over her, dark eyes concerned. Or so it appeared. There was no reason for him to be concerned about her, no reason at all.

She shook her head, unable to take her bright eyes off his lean face. 'What are you doing here?' she whispered, as he began to rub her back with the towel.

'Your Father and I had . . . a difference of opinion about something. We spent so long arguing it wore us both out. As I'm alone at Blair Place he invited me to stay for the rest of the weekend. We can finish our argument in peace later this morning,' he went on, a grim note in his voice.

Juliet lifted a puzzled face to his, and he groaned.

'What's the matter?' Juliet's voice sounded, even to her, as if it came from far away. As if it might belong to some disembodied being sharing the room with them.

'Nothing's the matter!' Brook replied, harshly. 'Your back is dry. I'd better leave you to dry the rest.'

Juliet opened her mouth to protest, but he'd gone, the door closing silently behind him.

She lay back against the pillow, uncaring of the damp towels. His hands were warm and caring on her back, his touch a tender one. There had been nothing untoward in his handling of her. For a few minutes it had seemed that he cared. Juliet languidly finished drying, climbed into bed and, with the thought that Brook cared uppermost in her mind, she slept.

The fragrant smell of eggs and bacon greeted Juliet when she crept downstairs later, much later, Sunday morning. Mrs Snowden couldn't be back so soon? She must be. All Father ever managed was toast. He didn't seem to know what a frying-pan was for!

But Brook Wentworth was slaving over the frying-pan, one of Juliet's own checked aprons around his middle. She tried to suppress her chuckle, but he spun round at some slight sound she made, and laughed at her.

Juliet's big eyes were fixed upon his dear face and suddenly he wasn't laughing any more. Deliberately he turned his back on her, and her face fell, the glow within died and was buried. Either he did not remember the tender scene of a few hours before—or he *did* remember and wanted to forget it.

Juliet rubbed her moist palms on the front of her jeans. The desire to reach out and touch him was strong just then. She saw the way the longish dark hair curled at the nape of his neck, and wanted to run her fingers through it.

Then she noticed that his sweater needed darning. There was a hole just above the right elbow. Even if he didn't want to know her this morning she could still perform that little service for him. Shyly, she offered, but he shrugged, his face cold, bleak.

'Thanks, but Gemma will do it.'

Juliet bit her lip, savagely, wanting to feel the pain. But nothing could obliterate the other pain, the anguish, the plain jealousy. Gemma. All paths led back to her in the end, and Juliet knew she couldn't take any more.

CHAPTER NINE

STUDY block was over now, and the Christmas holidays loomed. One whole week, ending on Boxing Day, then Juliet could get back where she was happiest—on the wards, with the patients.

It was hospital policy that nursing students did not work paid overtime if it could be avoided, but Juliet's offer to work voluntarily on a geriatric ward was eagerly accepted.

Her father and Muriel Snowden were married a few days before Christmas, a simple register office ceremony, and Juliet dutifully went along. Mrs Snowden looked very smart in a french navy dress and jacket, Dr Reed immaculate as always in a dark grey suit. Only a few close friends were there, including Brook Wentworth.

Brook was alone and Juliet longed for a few minutes with him, but he apologised for not staying for the informal reception afterwards. He was spending a day or two with friends, he explained to her father, giving Juliet no more than a brief nod. With Gemma? Juliet wondered, but supposed she must still be away. That left Rosalind Paice.

Eaten with curiosity, and with a heart near to breaking, Juliet fell back on her vivid imagination. Yes, he was taking Sister Paice with him. They were off to Paris for a pre-Christmas break. She could see it all . . .

Disconsolately, Juliet walked to Westdean, the female geriatric ward, the day after the ceremony. How cold and empty Five Gables was without her father. Juliet felt very lonely, but knew there was an element of self-pity in her loneliness. A spell with the old ladies would soon put her right!

Sister Charlesworth on Westdean ward was very tall and thin, with greying hair and an abrupt manner, but she had kind blue eyes, Juliet decided, so perhaps her bark was worse than her bite!

Sister got one of the auxiliaries, May Curtiss, to show her around and find jobs for her. Juliet would be treated more or less as an auxiliary during the time she spent there. She didn't intend going in every day, of course, because geriatric nursing was very hard on the feet and she wouldn't be having another holiday until the summer.

There were thirty-eight beds and the ward was always full, May told her. As might be expected, there were a lot of cardiac patients, often suffering from some kind of chest infection as well.

The geriatrician believed in getting the old folk up as quickly as possible, and much of Juliet's time was spent walking patients, either up and down the ward or around the big, sunny day-room. In addition, Westdean, a ground-floor ward, was blessed with a verandah, and the ladies liked to sit there, chatting or reading. One or two were able to knit, but a great many, Juliet found, had fingers crippled by arthritis. They were always bemoaning the fact they couldn't do all the things they used to, that they couldn't give their washing a good scrub was a frequent complaint!

She was sitting in the dayroom playing snakes and ladders with two of the old ladies when Michael O'Boyle found her.

She glanced up, eyes wary. After the unfortunate episode in Gemma's bathroom, Juliet had gone off the young doctor.

He seemed unaware of her coolness, and beamed at the ladies. 'So, I've tracked you down at last, Juliet! Someone said you were on holiday so I called at your dad's house. He must be away—or he saw me coming and hid under the table!' he laughed, and Juliet's mouth twitched.

She wasn't yet ready to forgive him, so managed not to laugh. 'He got married—to the housekeeper. They're away.'

'Oh! Left Juliet Cinderella all alone, have they?'

Perhaps it was her imagination, but she thought she detected sympathy in his voice, and she bridled: 'I am *not* Cinderella! Did you want something, Dr O'Boyle? Because it's my turn with the dice and you are holding up the game!'

He chuckled, not at all put out by her manner. Instead of going away as she had hoped, he sat down beside Mrs Shaw, an eighty-year-old, and patted her hand gently. 'Tell me about yourself then, Mother. Why haven't we met before?'

His dark head was bent towards the patient, his charm working on her just as it sometimes did on Juliet, and, smiling, she rattled the cup holding the dice. No one was perfect. Dr O'Boyle had his good and bad points just like anybody else. It was idle to compare him with Brook Wentworth. *He* certainly was no angel!

Without seeming to try, Michael O'Boyle soon had Juliet's Christmas plans out of her. He was going to be off-duty on Christmas Day. Why, he asked directly, could they not spend the day together?

'Because I shall be here,' Juliet said firmly, then yelped as her counter had to slide down a huge, curly snake. 'And I was nearly there,' she said sadly.

Mrs Cotton patted her hand. 'Don't worry, dear. Once you're down the only way is up.' The old lady rattled the dice enthusiastically.

She was right, Juliet thought in surprise. When you are at rock-bottom, there *is* no way to go but up. As far as Brook was concerned, little Juliet Reed no longer existed. He didn't care, he had others. So, Juliet would pick herself up and start climbing the ladders again. Make a new life for herself. It was juvenile to pine for a man she clearly could not have. Apart from being several years older than her, he was also her senior in position. Consultants didn't marry junior student nurses. They weren't in the same league.

Smiling bravely, Juliet said, yes, she would be very pleased to spend part of Christmas Day with Dr O'Boyle, and was rewarded by a lovely smile.

She *would* carve out a new life for herself, and damn Brook Wentworth!

Of course it didn't work. She ought to have known it couldn't possibly work. There was no one else quite like Brook Wentworth. There never could be a substitute. She loved him and there was nothing else to be said on the matter. Michael O'Boyle was fun. But he wasn't the man she loved.

Christmas Day was hectic. She and Michael went for a

brisk walk before lunch, which they had in the staff canteen. The roast turkey tasted almost home-cooked. Juliet, who thought she would spend Christmas pining for her father, did no such thing. She barely thought about him, beyond raising her canteen cup in a silent toast to him and Aunt Muriel, as her step-mother wished to be called.

Juliet and Michael helped feed the ladies on Westdean ward. He was a great success with them, and their reactions brought a tear to her eyes. He loved old ladies—*all* ladies, she corrected herself. Michael was a born charmer. She only wished he had the same effect on her!

Christmas evening they went to a party in the Nurses' Home. Juliet, who hated crowds and loud noises, wouldn't have enjoyed it if it hadn't been for Michael. Enthusiastically, he joined in every party-game, making sure that Juliet did, too.

The dancing afterwards was rather wild and woolly, but she enjoyed that. Dancing several inches away from her partner suited her. She recalled the way Andy had danced with her, the closeness, the feeling of being stifled, and shuddered. She wondered what it would be like dancing with Brook. If, in fact, he ever danced. She closed her eyes, willing him into view. He would never come to a nurses' party, of course, but she could dream, couldn't she? And she had her memories—of strong yet gentle hands drying her, of the excitement that his touch engendered, of the sadness in the depths of those dark, *weary* eyes.

Oh, Brook! her heart cried. I *love* you!

Unaware that her expressive face was showing her

anguish, Juliet allowed Michael to kiss her under the mistletoe. She clung to him, unashamedly, but in her mind it was another man's arms she sought, another man's kiss . . .

Michael drew back, eyes serious for once, then he put a huge hand under her chin and made her look at him. 'It isn't going to work, is it? Having a nice, easy friendship with me? You're miles away, Juliet.'

Dimly, she heard the background music, the shouts of laughter all around as the others enjoyed the party, but they might have been alone in the corner, for all the notice anyone took.

'I'm sorry, Michael. Truly I am,' sad-eyed, she met his gaze.

'You're surely not carrying a torch for old Dark and Dismal?'

'Who?' Surprised, she edged out of his arms.

'Dark and Dismal is what I call the boss. Mr Brook Wentworth. He's too old and too serious for you, Juliet, my darling. Too *intense*. You need someone—a lad like myself—to cheer you up, bring you out of your shell. He's not for you, Juliet.' He shook her, gently, as if the physical contact gave his words more emphasis.

He was right. Brook Wentworth wasn't for her. That didn't stop her wanting him, though. 'Possibly I like serious people around me,' she hedged, unwilling to admit her feelings to Michael.

'You live in wonderland, Juliet. A land where the goodies are good, the baddies are bad. People aren't like that. There isn't a chivalrous knight waiting to carry you off to his castle, put you on a pedestal and worship you ever after. Life has to be *lived*, my girl. This knight you're waiting for is more likely to drag you off to his house, put you in bed and make a woman out of you!'

'Michael!' Blushing, Juliet made to flee, but his long, ape-like arms stopped her.

'Don't run away from the truth, Juliet. If you're wanting this man, go out and get him! Offer him what he wants. Then maybe he will make you happy for a wee while until the next passing fancy comes along,' he added, drily.

His hands were hurting her but his words hurt even more. *Was* she a naive little girl, just waiting for some gallant knight to put her on a pedestal or to carry her off to church, dressed in virginal white? *Wasn't* that what she wanted? Could she do as Michael suggested—fling herself at Brook, offer herself on a plate, enjoy a brief affair?

Tiredly, she shook her head. She loved him but could not tolerate a cheap affair, even if such liaisons were fashionable. She *wanted* a white wedding, she wanted to go to her marriage bed unsullied, bright-eyed and wondering. If you had umpteen affairs what was the use of marrying?

'I *am* waiting for a handsome knight to carry me off to his castle and marry me,' she admitted, with a self-derisory laugh. She lifted her face to Michael in appeal. 'Is that so very stupid of me?'

Michael dropped a brief, brotherly kiss on her pretty mouth. 'No, it is *not* stupid. I think it's lovely, really I do. I only hope there *is* a handsome knight who is worthy of you, Juliet. Don't waste yourself on Brook Wentworth.'

Juliet covered her ears with her hands. She would not

listen to any more hurtful remarks about the man she adored.

With an exasperated sigh, Michael released her. Soon they were on their way to Juliet's home in his old car. It was painted bright green with a big white heart on the boot, and just about summed Dr Michael O'Boyle up—happy-go-lucky, living only for today. And unwilling to become serious about *any* girl—least of all little Juliet, who wanted a man she could lean on, a knight to whom she could look up, respect.

'It's getting very dark these evenings,' Michael said as he helped her out, and she smiled.

'It is generally dark in December!' she chided. 'But hasn't it been a gorgeous Christmas Day! So mild and sunny. It's hard to believe it *is* Christmas. I wanted snow,' Juliet went on, almost to herself, and Michael shook her, gently.

'There you go again! Because a white Christmas is traditional and romantic you must have one!'

Juliet laughed, seeing the funny side of it. 'Like a white wedding!' she giggled, and Michael joined in.

'I suppose you must have orange-blossom to hold your long white veil in place?' he teased.

'Oh, yes! And I'll have six bridesmaids, and carry a bouquet of white roses!' She laughed again, because if she hadn't, she would have burst into tears.

'It isn't the rose-growing season,' a bleak voice broke in, and the laughter died in Juliet's throat.

Brook Wentworth appeared out of the darkness, his wide mouth a harsh line. He was seething with a cold, *controlled* fury. Even in the meagre light from Michael's headlights Juliet could see that, and she shuffled from one foot to the other uneasily. *Now* what had she done?

To his credit, Michael O'Boyle stood his ground, unwilling to leave the tender-hearted Juliet with the man he had described as 'dark and dismal'.

'Good evening, sir,' Michael said, politely, but Brook barely grunted in reply. His intense gaze was on Juliet, and, frightened, she moved closer to Michael.

'Do you want something, Mr Wentworth? I mean, Father is still away,' Juliet quavered, feeling the strength from Michael's protective hands flowing through her.

'Your father asked me if I would keep an eye on you over Christmas. See that you weren't lonely,' the surgeon said, softly.

'Did he? It was nice of you to come to see me!' Juliet brightened. He wanted to be sure she was safe and sound!

'I would have come before but I forgot. It was only about an hour ago I remembered you, Nurse Reed.'

The words dropped into her happy mood like stones. Each word was said deliberately, she felt, as if he was underlining the fact that he had forgotten. She was of so little importance that he hadn't remembered her until Christmas Day was nearly over!

Her mouth made a small 'O' of disappointment, but she uttered no sound. It was her way to keep heartache to herself and she wasn't about to change.

Michael shuffled his feet awkwardly. 'We've spent most of the day at the D.G.H., sir. Helping with the old people. Juliet goes to Westdean ward after the weekend.'

'Oh?' Brook's voice was cold, disinterested, and Juliet

balled her small fists, only he couldn't see that, of course.

'I'm sorry you have had a wasted journey, sir,' she säid, politely. 'Have you been waiting long?' Deliberately, she kept her voice cold and unfeeling. She just hoped he *had* been waiting a long time.

'No. Not long,' he replied, and Juliet wondered how she was going to get rid of him, for he showed no inclination to move. She wondered how he'd got there but realised, as before, that he must have parked his car around the back where there was more space.

Should she invite him in for coffee? She had been about to offer Michael some, so . . .

'Would you both like some coffee?' she asked, directing her words to Brook Wentworth, and he grunted assent.

She turned to Michael, but he declined, and she opened her mouth to protest. He couldn't possibly leave her alone with Brook!

But he did. 'Sorry, Juliet, but I'm on early duty tomorrow. Can't expect *two* days off, you know. Be good and remember what your Uncle Mike told you.'

Mournfully, she watched him get into the colourful old car. He waved a hand in salute as the tyres crunched on the gravel.

Juliet listened until the sound of his car could be heard no more. The night settled back into silence, and Juliet shivered.

'Did you say you wanted some coffee before you go?' Perhaps he would refuse now that they were alone.

'If it's too much trouble, of course . . .'

He left the sentence unfinished, and Juliet felt wretched, as he had intended her to. 'Of course it isn't any trouble,' she said, untruthfully, as she led the way indoors.

The cold, silent house shrieked at her. It seemed to be saying, 'Go away, go away, you don't belong!' It was an eerie sensation and Juliet shivered again. A frisson of—not exactly fear, but unease, made its way along her spine.

No, she didn't belong at Five Gables any more. She belonged wherever Brook was.

'The central heating helps, anyway,' Brook commented.

'It's not that warm, though. I feel very cold,' Juliet said in a small voice. The hearth was laid with logs and coal. She'd done that in the morning before going out, but it was far too late to light the fire now. A log fire was welcoming. Juliet hadn't realised how much she was missing her home comforts, a blazing fire always waiting for her, the welcome from the lighted windows, the hot, if over-seasoned, meals.

'Penny for them?' He stood very close, just behind her, and she imagined she could feel his warm breath fanning her cheek.

'I . . . I was thinking how much I miss the log fire,' she admitted. 'It's always well alight when I come home.'

'Home comforts are very pleasant, but not essential, Juliet. We can survive without them.' He moved to the hearth and leaned, with one hand on the ornate mantelpiece, staring down at the lifeless wood.

'I expect you're used to doing without home comforts,' Juliet said, thinking of the bleakness of Blair

Place. 'I'll put the kettle on.' She disappeared into the small, bright kitchen, lit the oven because she was hungry and fancied a bite of supper, then filled the kettle.

She knew when he came into the room even though she was busy at the stove. Even without the masculine, citrus tang of his aftershave, she would have known. Her muscles tensed of their own accord, but she carried on with the small, mundane tasks, pretending she didn't know. All the time she was aware, waiting for the tiger to pounce, knowing such an attack was inevitable.

'Juliet.' His voice was husky.

'Yes?' Deliberately, she carried on making the coffee. She stirred a teaspoonful of sugar into Brook's cup, remembering to put extra coffee in because he liked his strong.

'Congratulations. On your engagement, I mean.' There was a pause, but Juliet was too startled to speak. Sensing there was more, she waited.

'A big white wedding complete with orange-blossom,' he said, almost to himself. 'When is it to be?'

She met his gaze, but his eyes were hooded, and she didn't know what thoughts were milling around his mind. 'I . . .' She stopped as she was about to explain his mistake. No! Let him believe that she was marrying Michael O'Boyle. He had Gemma and Ros Paice, didn't he? Let him stew!

'I don't know. No plans have been made yet,' she replied, careful to be truthful.

The kettle boiled and she poured the water on the mixture of coffee and sugar. 'There. Nice and strong.'

Brook took the cups from her and stood aside for her

to precede him. The sitting-room seemed warmer now, and Juliet thankfully plumped down on the big settee. Tomorrow she must light the fire. The house just wasn't the same without it.

'He's a nice boy.' Brook spoke into the growing silence, as he absently stirred his coffee. 'Bit devil-may-care, though.'

'Yes,' she agreed. 'Help yourself to a biscuit. Mrs Snowden left me some shortbread.'

'Decent of her. I like shortbread.' He crumbled a small piece, put it in his mouth, then chewed, without tasting it, Juliet was sure. He was miles away. With Gemma, most likely.

'How is Gemma?'

'What? Gemma. She's a lot better. She's going to join a self-help group. Got big plans for going back on the stage.'

'She was an actress?' Juliet asked, surprised.

'A dancer. Nothing very grand. I don't suppose she ever got beyond the back row of the chorus!' Brook laughed, a sharp, unhappy sound, and Juliet's fingers itched to touch him.

'I'm sorry I can't help her. Be a friend to her, I mean,' Juliet said, sincerity shining out of her eyes. It was true. She was genuinely sorry for she had liked Gemma—until that episode in the bathroom.

'Yes, pity your young lad couldn't keep his hands off you. It rather spoiled Gemma's day. Brought back unhappy memories of her marriage.'

Juliet bit back the words she longed to throw at him. 'I'm sorry.' There was no point in quarrelling about it, but they did.

'He's had a few girls. Has he taken Alice in Wonderland down to the woods yet?' His dark gaze flicked over her, and she wanted to hit him.

'That, Mr Wentworth, is none of your business!' she flared. Why did *he* care? He was sticking his nose where it did not belong.

'He has.' It was a statement, not a question, and Juliet didn't bother to deny it. What was the use?

Brook finished his coffee in silence, had another piece of shortbread, then stood up.

Her eyes moved to his tall, lean figure of their own accord. Unashamedly she watched as he stretched, like a big, agile cat.

'You must come and see Gemma when she's discharged. She was asking about you.' He glanced down at her.

Gemma again. 'Yes, I'll try, but I do geriatrics next. It will be heavy work,' Juliet said, and he frowned.

'You do not *do* geriatrics! That's a horrible expression. You work on a geriatric ward. They are all individuals, Juliet. Never forget that.'

Annoyed, she scowled at him. 'I know that. I like old biddies. Though I suppose I shall have a lot of last offices to do,' she went on, sadly, recalling her first and so far, only, death.

'It's a privilege. The last service an attendant is privileged to perform for a patient.'

Juliet glanced up, surprised. 'That's exactly what Sister Paice said!'

'Did she? How is she, anyway? I haven't seen her for a week or two.'

'How should I know? She's your girlfriend, not mine!'

Juliet snapped, irritated because they seemed to spend their time discussing his girlfriends.

'Is she? Since when?' He sounded surprised.

'M . . . I heard that you and she were . . . were good friends,' Juliet prevaricated. She had been about to say that Michael O'Boyle had told her. 'She seemed fond of you when I was working on Arndale.'

'I doubt if Ros is fond of any man for long,' Brook chuckled. 'She's a love 'em and leave 'em type. Likes variety,' he went on, and Juliet thought: Like you. You and Sister are two of a kind.

'Never mind. You have Gemma,' Juliet said, sadly, and was appalled at the reaction she triggered off.

'Gemma! Don't ever speak of Gemma in that way!' he exploded, dragging Juliet to her feet. 'She's a lovely girl. She . . . she's had an extraordinarily hard life and don't you forget it!'

Anger blazed from those dark, compelling eyes and Juliet wondered why she had ever thought him cold. He still had hold of her wrist, and he moved his thumb slightly so that it rested on her pulse spot.

Momentarily, Juliet closed her eyes, feeling weak and faint. He must be deeply in love with Gemma for her innocent words to provoke such a reaction. How wonderful to be adored.

He must have read her mind, for he said, simply: 'I adore her. She's a burden sometimes, but no one is perfect, Juliet. There are a hell of a lot of grey tones in between.'

'I know that! Don't preach to me!' she flared, sick with a feeling she recognised as jealousy. She was beginning to hate Gemma and that made her feel even worse.

'I expect young O'Boyle is full of grey tones,' he went on, his thumb continuing its exploration of her pulse spot, and she tried to pull away.

'Please don't keep on about Michael! I . . . I love him!' Defiantly, her stormy eyes met his.

'A stormy sapphire sea,' Brook said, softly. He was trembling, and Juliet thought he must be cold, unless it was anger at her remarks about Gemma.

'If you're cold we . . . we can go into the kitchen,' she said, timidly, not wanting to destroy the fragile peace.

'Cold? No, I'm not cold, Alice-in-Wonderland. Far from it,' he replied, enigmatically, and she frowned.

'Well, then, if you'll excuse me,' she began, but he didn't release her.

In the hall, the chiming clock began to chime midnight and Christmas Day was over. As the last tone died away, his lips met hers in a tender kiss. He lifted his head and she saw the anguish in those black eyes. Michael's words came back to her—dark and dismal. Oh, no, he wasn't at all dismal! She loved him! Oh, how she loved him and she wanted his love in return.

Unthinkingly, she pulled his head down and pressed her sweet, rosebud mouth to his. His strong arms tightened about her, moulding her to his body.

Tremors shot through her as he picked her up and laid her on the thick, fur rug in front of the settee. It was an imitation bearskin, its deep furry pile warm and soft. Like swansdown, Juliet thought, lightheaded because she was in the arms of the man she loved, adored.

He leaned on her, pressing her down into the fur, and blissfully, she closed her eyes. She felt his lips on her eyelids, kissing them softly, then his mouth moved to her

neck. Her blouse had a deep, scoop-neck leaving most of
her neck and shoulders bare, and she moved ecstatically
as his lips explored her throat, her ears, then left a fiery
trail on their way down to the soft swell of her breasts.
She wasn't wearing a bra but she didn't remember until
too late.

His strong hands were warm on her bare arms, sending strange sensations through her body. Her legs were
like jelly as Brook's exploring hands moved down and
settled around her waist then pulled her blouse up and
began a slow, sensuous journey up to her small, firm
breasts.

'No,' she murmured, knowing it wasn't right. She,
Juliet, was going to save herself for her husband. She,
who had indignantly told Michael she wouldn't tolerate
a cheap affair—could this really be her? She must
escape, before it was too late. But it was already too late.
Their lovemaking had passed the point of no return.

'Please, no. Don't!' she managed, between small
gasps of pleasure as Brook's hands roved at will over her
slim body.

'Juliet,' he breathed, his voice sounding strained,
tense. She opened her eyes, almost afraid to look at him.
Those big black eyes were dark no longer; they were lit
by a feverish brightness. His breathing was laboured,
intense, then his hard mouth found hers again, and she
lost track of time.

He forced her mouth open and his tongue went on a
tour of exploration, quickly and deftly blazing new
trails, finding new ways of exciting and arousing her.

Her skirt was full and swirling, with a hidden zip at the
front, but it didn't take Brook long to find the zip and she

felt the skirt being pulled down over her hips. She must stop him, but she hadn't the energy. A weird lethargy overtook her, but she found strength enough to undo the buttons of Brook's crisp, white shirt.

He began to kiss her breasts while she was still fumbling with the shirt-buttons, and she gasped as desire leapt in her veins. He kissed her again, hotly, his lips demanding a response which she willingly gave. Her entire body was one flame, burning with love for him.

As if satisfied with her reaction, Brook turned his attention to the rest of her clothing and had already slipped her tights down before she woke up to what was happening. It was rape! She lashed out, catching the unsuspecting surgeon on the side of the face.

Brook swore and momentarily relaxed his grip. It was enough respite for Juliet who, sobbing with a mixture of shame and anger, scrambled up and held her clothes in front of her like a shield.

Bare-breasted and wearing only her pink lacy briefs, she screamed at him: 'Get out! I never want to see you again as long as I live!' The tears were streaming down her face, her luxuriant chestnut hair was bedraggled, and she felt cheap and used.

Twin spots of colour burned on Brook's cheeks as his contemptuous gaze swept over her. 'O'Boyle has done the necessary spadework!' he threw at her, as he began buttoning up his shirt. 'Why shouldn't I have a little of what's left?'

'Spadework?' She didn't understand, not at first. 'What has Michael got to do with it? At least he hasn't tried to . . . to rape me!' she spat, and he gave a derisive laugh.

'If you went to him willingly he wouldn't need to rape you, as you put it. Really, Juliet, you over-dramatise everything! Girls get themselves laid at regular intervals these days. Grow up!'

Methodically, he adjusted his trousers and replaced his necktie. 'I hope you found it satisfying. I suppose,' he went on, after he'd finished dressing, 'that you went to him all dewy-eyed and eager. I said that one day some boy would take Alice down the garden.'

A solitary tear washed its way down Juliet's left cheek, and Brook wiped it away. His touch was gentle, and Juliet found a wan smile from somewhere.

His eyes travelled down her body, from the skirt she was clutching to her breasts, to her long, slender legs. 'You'll catch cold, Juliet. Go and get dressed. I'll let myself out.'

She raised a hand to stop him, then let it fall to her side. What was the use? Clearing her throat, she called after him: 'You must have been hard-up for a woman, to want me. I'm sorry I disappointed you.'

She waited, for him to say that he wasn't hard-up or disappointed, that he had wanted *her*, Juliet Reed, and no one else.

His voice came to her faintly from the hall. 'I *was* hard-up, Juliet. I don't generally take other men's left-overs!'

The front door slammed and Juliet was alone. Slowly, she dressed then sank back onto the fur rug. Her fingers smoothed its pile. Then she curled up into a comforting foetal position and stared sightlessly into space as the bitter, salty tears flowed.

CHAPTER TEN

'JULIET?' Brook Wentworth's voice was unmistakable, and Juliet's hand shook as she cradled the telephone receiver to her.

'Yes, that's me,' she said, flippantly. Her heart was doing crazy things as she waited, breathless.

'I wonder if you would have dinner with me tonight?'

Her spirits rose. He wanted to take her out! But, no. She must be cool, offhand. After his despicable behaviour of a fortnight before, he had no right to expect her to forgive him. 'Well, I'm not sure,' she said, doubtfully. 'You aren't my favourite person at the moment.'

There was silence at the other end and for one awful moment Juliet thought he'd hung up. 'I see.' He spoke at last, his voice distant. 'If you expect me to come crawling with my tail between my legs like a naughty puppy—don't!'

Juliet had a mental picture of a spaniel with Brook's features and soulful black eyes crawling to her for a pat on the head, and she laughed. The laughter came bubbling up, and she couldn't stop.

'Juliet! For God's sake, what is the matter!' Brook sounded furious and Juliet laughed even more. The spaniel was snarling!

'A vision of you having your head patted!' she spluttered, but he couldn't see the joke.

'My *head* patted? Are you tipsy, Juliet?' He sounded worried, and Juliet tried to control herself.

159

'Oh, no. Quite sober, thank you. We were watching television.'

'We?' he asked, sharply, and Juliet smiled to herself. She was with Aunt Muriel, but she wasn't going to tell him that.

'Yes. There was an interesting programme on—about violence in the home.'

'I hope you enjoyed it,' he said, drily. 'Are you coming out or not, Juliet? I haven't the patience to argue.'

'Are you at a loose end, then?'

'As a matter of fact, I am. The evening stretches ahead interminably.'

Juliet sighed. She had certainly got the answer she deserved. 'Perhaps Sister Paice wouldn't mind enlivening your evening,' she said, petulantly. She waited, hoping he would dismiss the suggestion.

His next words angered her. 'I've already rung round the numbers in my little black book. They were all out or engaged elsewhere—except you, Alice in Wonderland.'

'Well, Alice in Wonderland *isn't* going to fill the gap!' she stormed. 'I can find plenty to do even if *you* can't.' She banged the receiver down. She had so wanted to go out with him, yet she'd turned on him like a harridan.

'Oh, Brook!' she murmured. Excusing herself and leaving Aunt Muriel to her television, Juliet fled upstairs.

Her room was even more crowded now, and there certainly wasn't room to swing the proverbial cat! As she'd suspected, Aunt Muriel, once she'd married Juliet's father, did not want Juliet's belongings in the bedroom, so room had somehow to be found for the tall, narrow chest of drawers and small dressing-table, both of which had belonged to the first Mrs Reed. The dressing-table just about fitted in, but the chest had to stand on the landing where Aunt Muriel complained about it almost daily.

It *was* in the way, even Juliet could see that, but her bedroom was so small and poky. Feeling sorry for herself, Juliet flung herself onto her narrow divan and tried to cry. But tears wouldn't come.

Instead, she closed her eyes and imagined Brook laughing down at her. Brook, with his eyes of night, his husky laugh, his sheer magnetism . . . Brook, who was attached to Gemma by a silken cord, a cord so firm he didn't notice when Gemma tugged it and drew him to her.

Angrily, she thumped the bed, wishing it was Brook's head she was pummelling. Why was he so blind? Couldn't he see that all Juliet's love was for him? No, of course he couldn't see it. And if she made a habit of attacking him verbally every time he approached her, he never would!

She was still spreadeagled on her bed when the doorbell rang. It was unlikely to be Brook, but even if it was she wasn't going down.

Aunt Muriel's chirpy tones couldn't be denied, though. Juliet was sitting up, staring miserably into space, when Muriel burst in. 'There you are! I told Mr Wentworth you'd be getting ready! Why aren't you?'

'I am *not* going out tonight!' Juliet said tightly, but Muriel wouldn't stand any nonsense.

'Of *course* you are, dear. Do you good. I've always thought you were too quiet. It isn't natural,' she sniffed.

'Off you go. I'll wait up for your father.'

Juliet didn't feel like starting an argument. No good
would come of it. If her step-mother wanted her out for
the evening she would go. There was no alternative.

Feeling like a stranger in her own home, Juliet had a
brief wash then put on the first outfit she found—a lilac
thick-knit suit, with cap sleeves and a high neck. Juliet
had fallen in love with it at first sight. At least Brook
wouldn't need to be ashamed of her.

She plaited her long hair and secured the plaits on the
top of her head with a slide. Determined to appear cool
and regal, she slowly descended the stairs, making-
believe she was a sophisticated twenty-five. *That* was the
age to be! No stepmothers to chivvy you out when you'd
much rather stay at home. No parents to nag, no curfew.
Why, she could stay out all night!

Wishing even more fervently that she was twenty-five,
Juliet sidled into the sitting-room and gave Brook a cool
smile as he stood chatting to Mrs Snowden.

'There you are, then!' Aunt Muriel cooed. 'Go out
and enjoy yourself, dear!' She turned to Brook and gave
him a sly dig in the ribs as Juliet watched, fascinated.

He surveyed Juliet, his eyes taking in the plaits and the
lilac outfit. She knew he preferred her in green or blue.
Well, too bad!

'Quite nice,' he commented, his fingers fastening
around her wrist like a vice. 'Come on. We don't want to
be late back.'

Seething, Juliet nonetheless allowed herself to be
marched to the car, where Brook saw her comfortably
settled in the front seat.

Mrs Reed waved and smiled as the car drew away, and

Juliet found that her nails were digging into the palms of her hands.

'Seems a caring little body.' Brook's voice broke into her dark thoughts, but she merely grunted.

'No need to be jealous of her, Juliet,' he said, sharply. 'She'll take care of your father. You won't always be there to keep him company.'

'No,' she agreed, prepared to be docile and compliant for the evening. She just hadn't the energy for a fight. Westdean ward wasn't heavy—it was impossible! By the end of her shift of duty, Juliet's feet were like balls of fire. They burned. There was no other word for it.

Naturally, she received lots of well-meaning advice on how to get over that—soaking them in hot water then rubbing with surgical spirit being a favoured remedy among the older nurses. Sister Charlesworth told her there was little she could do, though. It was simply a matter of time before her poor feet got used to the constant running about.

'Sulking, Juliet?'

'No! I'm weary!' she snapped, forgetting about being docile. 'I ache in every limb. It's all that lifting and the bed-baths and so on. Old ladies are so heavy!'

'True. Still, nurses are strong, muscular creatures. You'll soon develop muscles you didn't know you had.'

'Thanks! I don't want to be a female Mr Universe! Though they did mention my size when I applied,' she said, recalling the preliminary interview with the P.N.O. and the senior Tutor. 'They asked me if I had any experience of lifting,' she went on. 'Said there was a lot of heavy work in nursing, and did I think I was strong enough to cope.'

'I thought the days had gone when nurses were selected for their strength rather than their brain,' Brook commented, drily.

'It doesn't seem so. Though the little Filipino girls manage all right. And they are a lot smaller than me,' Juliet pointed out. 'It's technique that matters in lifting patients, not strength.'

'I didn't intend that we should talk shop,' Brook put in, and Juliet smiled.

'Perhaps we have nothing else to discuss,' she said, quietly, and he shot her a sharp glance.

'We can discuss Gemma,' he said, but Juliet shook her head, vehemently.

'Oh, no, we can't! I've suffered enough because of Gemma and her warped sense of humour!'

'Aha! That episode in the bathroom *was* her doing, then?'

Juliet felt awful. 'I didn't mean to tell you. I'm sorry.'

'Sorry? It's I who should apologise for believing it,' he said, and she gave him a sour look.

Brook apologising when it should be Gemma! Juliet noticed that he didn't blame Gemma.

'Is Gemma coming out soon?' It was as well to be forewarned, Juliet thought.

'Yes, in a day or two, I believe. Did I tell you about the alcoholic self-help group?'

'Yes,' she said, distantly. If Gemma was going to help herself, all well and good, but Juliet didn't intend to get involved.

'I must fill you in with a few details over dinner,' he said, apparently not noticing her lack of interest. 'During your training you'll learn about alcoholism and about drug abuse, you know. And you'll meet both when you do A and E. It can be pretty nasty there on a Saturday night. I can remember it from my casualty days, and I doubt that things have changed much.'

Juliet hadn't thought about A and E. In any case, it was a long way off.

They drew in at a small, isolated restaurant with a nearly full carpark. Juliet looked about her with interest as they walked to the door, where soft lights welcomed them.

As they made their way through the crowded cocktail bar, she heard music and was delighted to find a small ensemble playing quite near the table to which the waiter directed them. He deftly removed the 'reserved' sign before smilingly presenting them with the menu.

Juliet lifted a brow. So Brook had reserved a table, had he? He was sure enough that one of his cast-off flames would accompany him. She wished now that she'd turned him down. Of course, she *did* turn him down, now she came to think of it. It was Muriel's doing that she was here at all. Hopefully, the food would be worth it.

It was. After Juliet had pointed out that she couldn't eat any food that was highly seasoned, she allowed Brook to choose for her. After some thought, Brook chose the smoked salmon to start with, for both of them, then licked his lips as he pondered over the main course. 'You're in for a treat tonight, Juliet,' he smiled, but only with his mouth. 'Rupert's food is well-known. He's noted for his international dishes.'

Juliet, remembering the curries she'd eaten at home,

nodded and tried to look happy. Please don't let him pick curry! she thought.

When the waiter had gone, Brook told her firmly to eat her salmon and try to look as if she was enjoying her evening out. 'You're such a sour puss I wonder I *ever* invite you for a meal!' he said, sharply, and she gasped at the injustice of it.

'I didn't ask to come here,' she retorted, their heated exchange drowned by the gipsy violin music. 'Anyway, it's only the second time you've asked me out for a meal.'

'Second? Is it? I don't remember inviting you out before.'

'One lunchtime when I was still on Arndale,' she reminded him. 'You asked me out and we had omelette and chips.'

He looked astonished. 'Omelette and chips? *Chips*? Are you sure, Juliet? I never eat chips,' he said, firmly.

'You did *that* day,' Juliet replied, equally firmly. 'We didn't have time for a full meal so we settled for omelettes. You wanted to talk about Gemma, if you remember.'

His face cleared. 'Of course! Yes, we did have omelette and chips. I'd forgotten.'

Naturally, anything to do with Juliet was easily forgotten! But she didn't say anything, merely glowered. Then the main course arrived and Juliet forgot how tiresome Brook was. It smelled delicious. Whatever it was, Brook was having the same.

'What is it?' she asked, sniffing appreciatively.

'Chicken, basically, with red wine and cream. Plus lots of vegetables.' He laughed at her evident delight. Then there was silence and peace for a while as they did full justice to the superb meal.

'About Gemma,' Brook began, as he cleared his plate, and Juliet's heart sank. The fragile peace dissolved. It took just that one word—Gemma.

'That was a delicious meal,' she said, quietly, hoping he would be sidetracked.

'Good. Glad you enjoyed it.'

A choice of sweet proved difficult and in the end Juliet settled for strawberry ice-cream. They were at the coffee stage before Brook returned to the subject of Gemma.

Juliet sat, eyes half-closed, replete and happy. They hadn't argued for at least fifteen minutes. Indeed, they hadn't spoken much at all, which was as well.

To her surprise, Brook had waved away the wine waiter, then, apparently realising that Gemma wasn't with him, he'd ordered wine after all. The combination of wine, good food and sweet music was having an enervating effect on Juliet. She just wanted to curl up, preferably in Brook's arms, and sleep.

'Sure you wouldn't like a French coffee?'

'Hm? Oh, no. No, I really couldn't, thank you.' Her eyes shone with gratitude and Brook seemed unable to drag his gaze away from her small, pert face. His expression was sad, a trifle wistful, and Juliet wondered if he was making-believe that she was Gemma—a Gemma who could be allowed alcohol without becoming ill again.

'Will you come to see Gemma when she's back home?' he asked, his tone half-apologetic, eyes sombre.

Juliet couldn't refuse, not when he looked at her like that. The sad spaniel-puppy expression in his eyes tore her in two. At that moment she was prepared to do anything for him, just to hear his husky laugh again, and see him smile.

'Of course I'll come, but . . .' But what would they talk about? 'After the bathroom episode, I doubt that we shall have much to discuss,' she pointed out.

He looked defeated, and, impulsively, she put her hand over his and squeezed. 'I'll find something to discuss with her, don't worry.'

Brook covered her hand with his own, and gave her a tender smile. So tender that for a moment she thought he cared, then she pulled herself together. This—the superb meal, the whole evening, tender smile and all—was solely for Gemma's benefit. *She* was the one to gain, not Juliet. Though, just for a moment, she pretended that he *did* care. She was Alice in Wonderland again, exploring a strange, tempting new world. All of a sudden she felt much older than her nineteen years. *She* was the mature woman, Brook the young boy who needed help, comfort.

'Thank you, Juliet,' he said, simply. 'You look good tonight,' he added, to her pleased astonishment. 'Don't tell me the sophisticated outfit is for my benefit?'

She blushed, feeling nineteen again. 'I . . . I *like* this suit,' she said, defensively. 'It's a pretty colour.'

'So it is.' He leaned forward and planted a kiss on the top of her nose, and she just stared, open-mouthed.

That husky chuckle broke from him. 'Come on, Alice. Time to go home.'

Sighing, she rose. Yes, get Alice home to bed. She has agreed to do what you want, so why waste any more time?

Her mood sombre, Juliet followed him to the car. The night air was bitterly cold and sleet was falling.

'Nasty,' Brook commented, hurrying her into the car. 'No snow yet, then? Didn't I hear you tell young O'Boyle that you wanted a white Christmas?'

Juliet nodded. 'It's too late now, anyway. Snow wouldn't be the same now.'

'Nonetheless, I think snow is what we will get before the month's out.' Brook set the car in motion and the drive was completed in silence. Indeed, Juliet was more than half-asleep, and was irritated when Brook shook her, none too gently.

'Time to get up, Alice,' he laughed.

Her legs had gone to sleep, so he gently manoeuvred her out and carried her into the house. Bemused, Juliet clung to him, feeling his warmth fill her. Then she found that it wasn't her home, it was his!

She turned her surprised gaze at him.

'It's all right. I'm not kidnapping you. Thought we could have a nightcap before I take you home. The night is young, Alice.'

'I wish . . .' she began but was effectively silenced as his mouth came down on hers.

He unlocked the dark, silent house and set her down. 'In there.'

Juliet, still shaken by the kiss, was about to protest that she wasn't going into Gemma's den, but catching hold of her wrists with effortless ease, he pulled her firmly through the middle door, along a short passage-way and into a huge, stone-flagged kitchen. A bright, warm room filled with all kinds of labour-saving gadgets.

'There. Sit yourself down and I'll make some coffee.

Unless you want something stronger?'

'No, coffee will be fine, thank you,' Juliet replied, dazedly, wondering where Gemma was.

'There's a cloakroom back through the passage, next to Gemma's den, if you want a wash and brush-up,' he said, busying himself with the coffee.

Juliet, glad to get away from his disturbing presence, found the room. Quickly, she wiped her makeup off with a moist pad, then plunged her face into the cold water, trying to revive herself. Her face burned, her whole body, too.

She stared at her reflection in the big oval mirror over the wash-basin. A wan face stared back, devoid now of cosmetics. A clean, well-scrubbed face, very ordinary, she thought.

Without thinking, she undid the slide and gently unplaited her hair, letting the rich tresses free. A quick comb-through was all her hair got as she walked slowly and thoughtfully back to the kitchen—and Brook. What, she wondered, happens next?

The kitchen was apparently a breakfast room, too, as a table and four stools were set in an alcove. Apart from that, the room was sparsely furnished, except for the kitchen units along one wall.

Juliet went to investigate, opening drawers, peering into cupboards, quite forgetting that Brook was only an acquaintance and she had no right to do so.

The electric cooker, with its rotisserie, fascinated her, then came a series of work-tops, while at the opposite end stood a big automatic washing machine, a spin-drier and a tumble drier. The freezer was in the big, walk-in larder, Brook told her, his gaze amused as Juliet explored.

'It's an upright. Easier to get into than the chest-type,' he commented. 'We have a fridge, as well—just a small one. The larder's cool, anyway.'

'It's wonderful! Just the sort of kitchen I always wanted!' Then Juliet blushed, thinking he would read more into her remark than she intended.

'You blush a lot,' Brook chuckled, watching her go even redder.

'It's the hormones!' Juliet said, sharply, as the tide of colour showed no sign of receding. 'Teenagers *do* blush a lot. It's something we grow out of,' she said, her eyes meeting his unflinchingly.

'Ah, yes. Funny things, hormones,' he drawled, amusement still in his voice. 'Sit down if you have finished searching my cupboards. Coffee's up. *Real* coffee,' he emphasised, setting the tray down on the table.

Feeling small, Juliet did as she was told, then stared down into the cup.

'What do you know about Delirium Tremens, Juliet?'

Aghast, she looked up. 'I don't know anything about it! I'm tired!'

'I brought you here to wake you up a little.' Brook sounded vexed, and Juliet rested her chin in her hands as she settled down for the lecture.

'It's an alcoholic psychosis,' Brook began, stirring cream into his coffee.

Great, she thought. It's eleven-thirty at night and he wants to discuss alcoholism.

I'd much rather be in your arms, she mused, a half-smile curving her mouth. If only he knew!

'D.T.s is a confusional state,' Brook continued, softly,

as Juliet's eyes began to close, and she heard no more.

When she awoke a cold, grey light was filtering in through the open curtains.

Confused, Juliet sat up, her anxious gaze taking in the big bed, the unfamiliar room. Where on earth *was* she?

She put her head in her hands, trying to remember. Was it early evening now or morning?

Brook. Ah, yes. Brook boring her to sleep with delirium tremens!

It must be morning! Juliet thought. It *is* morning or I've been out all night! 'Oh!' she murmured aloud. Father will kill me. And where is Brook?

Thankfully, the consultant wasn't curled up next to her. She appeared to have spent the night alone, which was something to be thankful for. Or was it? Juliet mused, searching for her clothes.

She found the light switch eventually, and closed the curtains. It was far too dark to see. Her suit, jacket and shoes were in a neat pile by the radiator. She stared down at what she was left with, a minute bra and briefs set and her slip. Why, he'd even removed her tights!

Warm colour flooded her face as she pictured his hands on her body, stripping her. However could she face him this morning?

It was just before eight o'clock, and a groggy Juliet went in search of the bathroom. She might as well wash before she faced Brook.

The bathroom adjoined the bedroom and she guessed it was Brook's. A big bathroom cabinet stood on the window-sill, and, curious, Juliet opened it was found it full of masculine items. Yes, there was that tangy after-shave she liked so much.

Juliet had a shower, being careful to lock the door first, then quickly dressed. Greatly daring, she splashed after-shave behind her ears and on her throat and wrists before going downstairs.

Still not decided whether to be angry with Brook, Juliet ran him to ground in the kitchen. He was casually dressed in brown cord slacks and a checked shirt, busy with a frying-pan.

'Morning, Alice,' he said, cheerfully, laughing at her mutinous face. 'I hope you're on late duty today.'

'I am,' she replied, coldly. 'You shouldn't have let me sleep here,' she went on, ignoring the tempting array of food on the table. She was hungry, but wasn't prepared to admit it.

'I didn't have the heart to wake you, Juliet. You sleep like a kitten, curled up in a ball, snoring gently,' he teased, and she flared up.

'I don't snore! You're hateful! Hateful!' she flung at him, then, to her shame, she began to cry. Big, choking sobs that she couldn't control. She, quiet, self-contained Juliet, who never cried in front of others! Her personality changed whenever she was with this man. Some chemistry in them both made her over-react, become a weepy violet, the type of girl she despised.

She turned her face to the wall, sobs shaking her slender frame.

'Juliet.' He spoke her name, softly, but she didn't want to hear him.

'I hate you!' she told the wall, then Brook exploded. One minute he was by the cooker, the next he was by her side, shaking her like a terrier shaking a rat.

'Shut up, Juliet! Do you hear me! Be quiet!' He shook

her again, and his hands were punishing the smooth flesh of her arms.

'Stop it, Juliet! Do you hear!' he snarled, and she tried to wriggle out of his grip.

'Please, don't,' she gulped. 'Just leave me.'

'That's something I can never do, my love,' he said, harshly, and Juliet's eyes widened in disbelief. She was hearing things!

He groaned. 'Juliet, do you know what you're doing to me? Do you *care*? I suppose,' he went on, bitterly, 'you would laugh if you knew the number of nights I've lain awake, just thinking about you.'

'Brook,' she said, wonderingly, still not sure that she was hearing him correctly.

'That sounds good. Say it again,' he murmured, enfolding her in his arms.

She smiled, puckishly. 'Brook,' she said, firmly. 'That's a nice name.' She snuggled herself closer, and he moaned, softly, a sad, despairing sound. Then he bent his dark head and kissed away the loneliness, the sorrow, the tears of despair that she'd wept over him. Happiness flooded over her. Brook loved her! He loves me, he loves me! her heart sang, as she responded to his lovemaking. If Brook loved her, that was all that mattered.

His warm hands moved sensuously over her body, then he gazed down at her. She longed to tell him she adored him, but the first words must come from him. He *did* love her. Wasn't he showing it in a hundred ways?

'Juliet. My sweet little Alice in Wonderland,' he murmured against her hair. 'If you only knew! It was touch and go whether you slept in that bed alone last night! I had to lock you in to protect you from myself.'

'Did you?' she asked, wonder shining out of her eyes. 'I wasn't locked in this morning. Kiss me again,' she demanded, winding her arms around Brook's neck. 'I like you to kiss me.'

Savagely he crushed her closer, and she could feel the urgent need in his body. 'What about O'Boyle? The man you're going to marry? Doesn't he have any say in the matter?' His dark eyes blazed with jealousy and fury, and Juliet smiled indulgently, meaning to tell him about his mistake.

'O'Boyle doesn't count,' she began, but got no further as his lips claimed hers. A savage, punishing kiss—the sort of kiss she imagined men gave to goodtime girls. Not what her romantic nature longed for.

His hands roamed at will, exciting yet repelling her. He pushed up her suit-top, his fingers, hard and cruel on her body.

'No-o. Brook, don't!' she cried, horrified, and he ground out, bitterly:

'Don't tell me lover-boy doesn't like to caress you? I believed in you,' he went on, turning from her, despairingly. His voice shook as Juliet tried to re-arrange her clothes. 'I called you Alice in Wonderland. But you threw yourself away on that Irish charmer! He plays the field, Juliet. How could you? Answer me!'

She backed away, terrified by the madness in his eyes. 'I haven't! He isn't my lover! He's just a friend, Brook. Please believe me! You . . . you came in on the tail end of our conversation on Christmas evening. He was making fun of me because I wanted a big white wedding

one day. With . . . with six bridesmaids!' she flung at
him, her face white.

'Oh, Juliet! Juliet, I'm sorry! Forgive me?' He looked
and sounded so wretched that Juliet nodded.

'Come and sit down.' He led her gently by the hand to
a rocking-chair she hadn't noticed before. He sat her
down and began to rock the chair soothingly.

'I must phone Father,' she began, but Brook shook his
head.

'I spoke to him on the telephone last night. Told him I
had trouble with the car and I would put you up for the
night. He won't be worrying,' Brook assured her, and
she relaxed, trying to forget the recent turmoil.

'That nice?' he murmured, his eyes searching her face,
and she managed to smile. It *was* nice. 'Anyone would
think you were jealous,' she said, quietly, and waited,
half-fearing a violent reaction from this pale, intense
man she loved.

'Perhaps I am,' he admitted, gruffly. 'Another man
getting what I want. I want you, Alice in Wonderland.'

Her heart fluttered. Want, not love. He hadn't said he
loved her. 'You've got Gemma. You don't need me.'

'Gemma.' He echoed the name softly, and Juliet was
torn asunder by jealousy.

'Yes, Gemma. Go to her with your . . . your fancy
words!' she cried.

'Listen, Juliet.' Brook stopped the rocking motion
and clasped her hands from behind the chair. 'I wanted
to tell you last night about her, but you fell asleep.'

'The D.T.s isn't the most interesting of topics,' she
said, drily, and he laughed, a husky, intimate laugh. She

turned her head, but still couldn't see him properly. 'Rock me again,' she demanded, and he obliged, setting the chair in motion and coming round to kneel in front of her.

He warmed her hands between his own, his expression sad. 'Will you hear me—without interrupting?'

She nodded. 'But don't take too long. I have to be on duty at twelve-thirty,' she reminded him.

'Hm. And then? When are your days off?'

Her face changed, and she could not conceal the dismay in her eyes. He mustn't know about her days off! 'I! . . . I'm not sure.'

Brook frowned. 'I thought rotas were arranged weeks in advance?'

'Yes, but . . .' She couldn't go on. She wouldn't lie to him, but neither could she tell him the truth—that she was going away with Andy Skilton. He might strangle her!

'Never mind, Juliet. I have no right to interfere in your private life,' he said, gruffly, 'but I want to tell you about Gemma.'

She waited, tensely, for him to tell her how much he adored his sister-in-law.

'Alcoholism is a serious disorder, Juliet. If you had ever seen anyone in a state of alcoholic delirium you would feel very sorry for them, no matter what your views on the subject. They can *die*, Juliet. Gemma has been near death's door once or twice.'

'Yes, but surely if she's had the D.T.s she would be afraid to drink any more in case she got it again when her alcohol was withdrawn?' It all seemed clear-cut to Juliet.

'It doesn't always work that way, my dear. Gemma

needs help to overcome her reliance on alcohol. This is what I've been endeavouring to provide.'

Juliet's heart leapt. Did that mean that his only interest in Gemma was as a doctor? He didn't love Gemma, after all? Eyes bright, she opened her mouth to assure him she understood, but he frowned and put a finger to his lips.

'You are supposed to be listening in silence, Juliet,' he reproved her, and she nodded, demurely.

'If only I didn't love her so much,' he went on, almost to himself, and Juliet's hopes crashed before they were even off the ground.

He loved Gemma. Therefore, he couldn't love Juliet. There was no hope at all, and she might as well go away with Andy. Find out what being a woman really meant. Heaven knows, Brook had taken her to the brink often enough, brought her to the edge of surrender, then stopped, leaving her oddly dissatisfied. Well, let him have Gemma! she cried, inwardly, not hearing a word Brook said. I wish him joy of her!

She jumped up, knocking aside Brook's restraining hands, then ran out of the house along the driveway and out into the road. It was a bitterly cold, grey morning and she'd left her jacket behind. No way was she going back there! She would run to keep warm.

It was a long way back to Garnhill and the warmth of Five Gables and Juliet couldn't run for long. Her steps slowed, faltered and finally stopped, and she was almost glad when she spotted Brook's Rover.

'Get in, you stupid bitch!' was the greeting she got from the man she loved, but Juliet was too cold to fight back. Swallowing her pride, she settled herself beside him, arms around herself, defensively. She wasn't going to listen to another word about Brook's love for Gemma. She wasn't!

Instead of going back to his house for her belongings, Brook drove her straight home, leaving her at the gate of Five Gables.

The car shot off into the distance, leaving a cold, hungry and bitter Juliet.

CHAPTER ELEVEN

'But, why?' Dr Reed's face was puce, and Juliet was fearful for his blood pressure. 'You have a perfectly good home here. Everything is done for you! Why, Muriel cooks some lovely meals!'

Juliet felt about an inch high and Muriel Reed's tears did nothing to help. 'I need to be on my own for a while, Father!' Juliet cried. 'I'm cut off here. If I live in, I can join in with the others more, make friends!'

'Live in one draughty little room when you've been used to a whole house!' Her father was aghast. 'Have you *seen* the accommodation in the Nurses' Home?'

Juliet nodded. 'Elma showed me her room once. It *is* small, but there is a big sitting-room and a quiet room, and plenty of bathrooms. It won't be too bad,' she assured him, and he and Muriel exchanged glances.

'I'm sorry you are jealous of me, dear,' Aunt Muriel said, stonily, 'but I can understand that you need to be among young people.'

'Does she?' Dr Reed turned to his wife, who nodded, emphatically.

'Let her try it for a few months. She will soon realise how well off she is here.'

Juliet's mouth tightened. She *would* miss the comforts of home, but she would have more room in the Nurses'

Home than she had now at Five Gables. She had dropped enough hints about being allowed a bigger bedroom, but to no avail.

Reluctantly and angrily her father gave in. Of course,
Juliet didn't need to ask his permission, but old habits of
obedience died hard. She loved her father and hated to
hurt him, but it was for the best. She needed to be free
and they needed to enjoy some time on their own.

She found she could not, after all, go away with Andy.
She had seen him a few times, enjoyed his company—
and his practised kisses. But a weekend away was never
really on. Andy wasn't Brook Wentworth.

She would be an old maid, living on her memories.
There could never be another Brook Wentworth and she
wasn't going to accept second-best.

'Just a minute!' The light tapping on Juliet's door was
insistent, and she hurried to open it. She *would* have a
visitor when she was working on her nursing care-study.

'Oh, Gemma!' Taken aback, Juliet could only stare as
a smiling Gemma strolled into Juliet's room and stared
about her, admiringly.

'This *is* pleasant, Juliet!' she trilled, big eyes shining.
'Quite a big room.'

'Yes, it's bigger than the bedroom I had at home,'
Juliet offered, not sure she was keen on the visit.

The older woman looked remarkably well, but she
always did, Juliet reflected. It was difficult to imagine
her fighting for her life, in the grip of hallucinations and
nightmares.

'Do sit down. Though there isn't anywhere very
clear.' Juliet hurriedly chucked some books off the

ottoman, and Gemma settled herself comfortably.

'Brook brought me. He wanted to come up, but that
dragon with three chins wouldn't let him!' Gemma
laughed. 'She apologised at least four times but wouldn't
budge. Rules are rules. No male visitors except fathers!'

'That *is* a sore point,' Juliet admitted. 'If we are
mature enough to run wards and save lives, then we
ought to be mature enough to have men friends in. It
doesn't necessarily mean we want to hold orgies!'

'Brook was furious! He turned on the charm, got
shirty, everything, but no go. Still, I wanted a word with
you alone.' Gemma leaned forward, and Juliet felt ill.
She must be about to say how much she loved Brook.
And Juliet didn't want to know.

'Look,' Juliet began, awkwardly, 'if it's about
Brook—I mean Mr Wentworth, I don't really think . . .'

'But I must tell you!' Gemma insisted, hazel eyes
filling with tears. 'He's done so much for me. Grant was
only his half-brother, you know. He . . . he wasn't quite
normal!' Gemma burst into tears, and Juliet hurried
over and put her arms around her, comfortingly. 'He
developed a brain tumour,' Gemma whispered. 'It
affected him mentally. He used to have terrible rages.'

'Please don't upset yourself. It isn't worth it, Gemma.
Your husband is dead and you can make a new life with
. . . with Brook.' Juliet choked on the word, and Gemma glanced at her out of tear-swollen eyes.

'No! Brook is like a brother to me. And I'm his dearly
loved sister. That's what I've been trying to tell you! He
doesn't seem to have made much of a job of telling you
himself.' She clutched Juliet's arm, eyes wide, appeal-
ing. 'I'm making a new life for myself, trying to live on

my own. You do believe me, don't you? I'm *such* a burden, I know!'

This confession brought on a fresh crop of tears, and Juliet soothed her again. Since that awful night she'd spent at Brook's house she had read up on alcoholism and knew such people were emotionally labile. Poor, poor Gemma. Brook didn't love Gemma as a man loves a woman but as a sister!

'I wish he loved me,' Juliet confessed, and Gemma gulped, and dabbed delicately at her eyes with a lacy handkerchief.

'But he does! I'm almost sure. Of course, he isn't the easiest of men to get through to, but I know he's fond of you,' Gemma assured her, and Juliet's heart grew wings.

Gemma was about to say more when there was a commotion outside, and someone hammered on Juliet's door. She hadn't locked it, and suddenly it was flung open.

Both girls gasped as Andy Skilton was hurtled bodily into the room, followed by a furious Brook Wentworth.

'Lover-boy tried to sneak up when the Warden's back was turned,' Brook said, bitterly, his contemptuous gaze raking Juliet, who flinched as though she'd been hit.

'He is not my lover-boy!' she cried, as Andy got groggily to his feet.

'I was nearly,' Andy put in, gingerly testing for broken bones. 'It wasn't my fault you got cold feet and wouldn't come for the weekend! I suppose you preferred *him*!' He gestured towards Brook, who looked as if he might spring any moment. 'Don't worry, I'm going!' Andy made for the door, Brook's intense, brooding gaze following him.

'I'm sorry,' Juliet said, in a small voice, and Brook's eyes blazed.

'Sorry! What use is being sorry? Now I have to get out without that old cat downstairs seeing me!' Brook banged the door behind him, and Gemma put a consoling hand on Juliet's arm.

All was lost now. Even if Brook had cared before, he wouldn't believe that Andy meant nothing to her.

Miserably, she picked up her textbooks and began to pile them neatly, just for something to do. She felt empty, bereaved.

'Oh, Juliet! I'll see Brook,' Gemma assured her. 'Tell him you love him, shall I?'

Juliet shook her head, vehemently. 'No! You mustn't! Please. Brook doesn't care. He'll believe what he wants to believe. All he's interested in is his career!' she snapped, unfairly, and Gemma went pale.

'He *is* ambitious. I suppose he didn't tell you?'

'Tell me what? That he is thinking of going to London sometime? I suppose that *is* the Mecca,' Juliet said, miserably.

'But it's all arranged. Just lately he's been *impossible*. You've no idea.'

Juliet had. She knew just how impossible the surgeon could be!

'He's going at the beginning of June. Right after the Bank Holiday. I thought he might have mentioned it?' Gemma's voice trailed away.

'That's all that matters, isn't it? Getting to the top of the tree,' Juliet reflected, sadly. 'I used to think doctors and nurses were dedicated, *caring* people, but those with ambition certainly aren't. Promotion is their god.'

'Don't judge Brook by some of the others,' Gemma urged her. 'He *does* care. He works long hours, you know.'

'I know,' Juliet whispered. 'I . . . I'm sorry about your husband, Gemma. I mean . . . having brain damage. I hope Brook's love will help you forget him.'

Gemma looked away. 'It wasn't easy. I lost my baby, too. And I did so long for one,' Gemma whispered. Then she got up and hugged Juliet.

'Don't give Brook up entirely. He's a man of strong feelings. Once he's got over this stupid misunderstanding, he'll be back. I only wish Grant had been half the man Brook is.'

Gemma let herself out quietly, and Juliet stared at the closed door. No, Brook would never come back. Let him go to London, further his ambitions. Let him become a rich Harley Street consultant if that was his heart's desire. But wherever he went, he would always carry Juliet's heart with him. And he would never know.

The fire-bell rang in the Nurses' Home two nights later, and a sleepy Juliet lay listening. She wasn't at all sure what it was, but heard movement from the other rooms.

Groggily, she put on her thick dressing-gown and slippers, then padded out into the corridor. There were people everywhere. Students in various stages of undress were milling about, then Sister Porter, the Home Warden, appeared, and called the girls together.

'Listen everybody! It isn't a fire, but there's an emergency. A train has crashed just outside the station, apparently.'

There was an excited buzz of conversation and Juliet's heart was in her mouth.

'We don't know the casualty-state yet, but trained staff are needed to help. You girls are also needed—to take their places on the wards.'

Sister Porter got the students into some sort of order and held a roll-call. Juliet was designated to help on Arndale as she'd been there before, so, quickly dressing, she sped over to the hospital.

It was three a.m. and only dim lights glowed in the main building. She hadn't yet done night duty so it would make a change. She was due on early duty that morning, though, and didn't think she would be much help when she finally staggered to Westdean after her night on Arndale, but she would try. She intended to work until she dropped if it would help the accident victims. *This* was what nursing was all about! The giving of yourself.

A warm glow filled her, as she tiptoed on to Arndale, where the trained night-nurse was preparing to leave to see what she could do for the train-crash victims. That left a capable third-year student, Pat Symes; an auxiliary, and Juliet.

'There isn't a lot to do but Mrs Elliott is rather poorly, so you might sit with her for a while,' Pat Symes instructed Juliet, who did as she was told.

Mrs Elliott was in her fifties, Juliet judged. She moved, restlessly in her sleep once or twice, but didn't wake, for which Juliet was profoundly grateful. The woman was nursed at the end of the ward nearest to the office, and the comforting dimmed light from the office shone out as Juliet sat.

She was called away eventually, to accompany Pat on her round. The surgical Night Sister looked in once, but hurried away when her bleeper went. Juliet gathered that there were a number of seriously injured casualties, who would need instant surgery.

Her thoughts went to Brook, fast asleep at Blair Place. He was missing all this—the fast-moving doctors and nurses who were, even now, fighting to save lives. Although Juliet had a much less spectacular role to play, she was needed, and it sent a warm feeling all through her.

Reports filtered back from time to time. There was only one death, but there were a great many requiring medical aid. All theatres were working flat out, and Juliet was glad she wasn't a theatre nurse. She just didn't think she could have coped.

About five o'clock, a call went out for more refreshments to go to those still working at the scene, and Juliet was delegated to go. It had been a quiet night on Arndale and the other two could cope without her now.

As Juliet was gingerly making her way down the embankment in company with several other juniors, a grimy hand shot out from the blackness and helped itself to a couple of sandwiches. Startled, she peered into the night and met Michael O'Boyle's big grin.

'Hello there, young Juliet! Keeping busy, then?'

Before Juliet could reply, the weary doctor had trudged away, and she hurried down to the train.

There were lights everywhere, illuminating the scene, and dozens of people working away.

From snatches of conversation, she learned that there

was still one man trapped in the wreckage, but Juliet knew she must not linger.

She hurried away, intent on getting more refreshments. A cup of tea worked wonders under such conditions. She wondered if her father was there, somewhere out in the blackness, but apart from O'Boyle, she didn't recognise anyone.

Although those on emergency duty were told that they didn't need to go to their own wards until late in the morning, Juliet felt able to take only four hours' sleep. Westdean ward was, as usual, under-staffed and Juliet was certain she could manage on four hours' sleep.

Once back in bed she fell asleep instantly, having prudently set her alarm, and a little after ten she presented herself to Sister Charlesworth, who also looked as if she'd been up all night.

There were only the two of them at first plus an auxiliary borrowed from elsewhere, and Sister worked as hard as Juliet, earning her undying respect. *That* was dedication to duty, Juliet thought, not the Brook Wentworth kind.

Just before lunch, Sister called her into the office to have a quick coffee, since she'd eaten nothing all morning. She simply hadn't been hungry but was now, and eagerly tucked into the ham and tomato sandwiches Sister had procured from somewhere.

'Mr Wentworth,' Sister said suddenly, pouring herself another cup. 'Isn't he a friend of your father's?'

'Well, yes, though I suppose Father must know *all* the consultants,' Juliet replied, puzzled.

'He's rather poorly, I hear. Been working flat-out like the rest of us. Collapsed from exhaustion.'

'He has? But . . . but I didn't know he had been called out!' Juliet's voice rose. Her Brook, lying ill somewhere!

'They all were. Dr Reed was there. Didn't you know?' Sister sounded surprised, so Juliet had to explain about living-in now.

'Ah, well. If you're living-in you can pop into see Mr Wentworth. He's in sick-bay. Give him some magazines. I simply haven't had a minute myself.' Sister produced three glossy magazines and thrust them into Juliet's arms.

Moments later, Juliet was on her way to Brook's room in the staff sick-bay. Her feelings were numb. Sister had said he was rather poorly. She wasn't a woman to exaggerate so he could be really *dangerously* ill! Suppose part of the train had fallen on him! Suppose . . . But her imagination was running away with her, she knew.

Juliet hesitated at the nurses' station, which was empty. Brook might be in theatre, fighting for his life in the very venue where he'd save scores of others!

'Oh, Brook, I love you!' she cried to herself, as a tear squeezed out and ran down her cheek. He was dying, and she had been so hateful to him!

Careless of what others might think, she pushed open every door she came to, and at last found Brook—he was sitting up in bed, with Sister Paice leaning over him solicitously.

And he was laughing up at her! The tears dried on Juliet's cheeks as she took in the situation. Two pairs of eyes turned, incredulously, upon her, and she fled, her heart irretrievably broken.

Juliet ran all the way back to Westdean, then she realised that she still held the magazines Sister had

promised Brook. Uncertainly, she gazed at them. If
Sister Charlesworth intended Brook to have them, then
have them he must, but she was not going back there to
be further humiliated!

After she recovered her breath, she stared sightlessly
out of the corridor window, and realised what a selfish,
immature fool she was. She ought to be glad that Brook
was all right. She'd conjured up a vision of him lying
paralysed or even dying, so she ought to be relieved that
he was so well.

Whether Sister Paice was simply a passing fancy or
not, Juliet must try to be pleased for him. He had
worked all night, saving lives, and *she* had been mentally
sneering at him because she'd thought him safe and
warm in bed all last night! Juliet Reed, she told herself,
firmly, you should be ashamed.

Even if Brook laughed and jeered at her, she would
deliver the magazines. If she was ever to be trained
nurse, capable of running a ward, she must grow up.
And now was as good a time as any.

Taking a deep breath, Juliet began to retrace her steps
along the corridor, vowing never to give in to deep
emotions again. She was nineteen and a half now, a
woman. She . . .

'It's those hormones, Alice,' a voice said, gently.
'They certainly work overtime, don't they?'

Brook was partly dressed, with trousers covering his
pyjama bottoms, but only his pyjama jacket keeping out
the cruel, February wind.

'Brook! You'll catch your death!' she wailed.

'You'll have to warm me up, Mrs Wentworth! Will
you?'

Disregarding the curious gazes of nurses passing, Brook cradled her to him. 'I love you, I always have. Ever since that day you brought me a cup of *very* weak coffee!' he chuckled. 'Say yes, Alice in Wonderland! Don't leave me now!'

His urgency communicated itself to her, as she gazed up, stars shining in her eyes. 'Oh, yes, please!' Then her face fell. Gemma! She'd forgotten Gemma.

'What is it, my little love?' Brook's dark eyes searched her face, and she whispered: 'What about Gemma?'

His face cleared. 'She's trying to go it alone, make a new life for herself, my dear. She might not succeed. Who knows? I love her as a sister. She went through hell, you know.'

Juliet nodded, understanding that Brook's love had to be shared. Gemma was a burden they would bear—together.

'She has moved out now, but we'll still keep a room for her, just in case. Hm?'

Juliet squeezed his arm, as, together, they strolled back to the sick-bay. Juliet's heart was full of tenderness for this man who had proved beyond all doubt that doctors *were* dedicated.

'Look, Juliet!' Her eyes followed Brook's pointing finger. 'Snow!'

'Too late for a white Christmas!' she laughed.

'You can still have a wedding in the snow, Juliet,' Brook murmured, his voice deep with emotion. 'Orange-blossom, six bridesmaids and all!'